KILL THE ENEMY

Indiw's toe claws ached with anticipation. The last time he'd disemboweled a Hyos, he'd been fighting beside Walter Falstaff, defending the carrier *Tacoma*. He hadn't gutted another Ardr since he'd been a child, but he well remembered the intense satisfaction of it. And, since he was now landed, it was once again legal for him to kill. . . .

Claws ready, he leaned across the cowling to do what had to be done. He saw the helmet and he struck reflexively at the intruder.

It was a stupid reflex. His claws slashed toward the pilot's throat and snagged in the tough flight suit.

With two claws caught in the neck seal, he saw the name blazoned across the front of the helmet. Raymond G. Falstaff, Jr., Pilot Lieutenant, *Tacoma*. . . .

It was Walter Falstaff's nephew.

BORDER DISPUTE

The return of Indiw, the alien pilot from Daniel R. Kerns's *Hero*.

Ace Books by Daniel R. Kerns

HERO
BORDER DISPUTE

BORDER DISPUTE

DANIEL R. KERNS

ACE BOOKS, NEW YORK

This book is an Ace original edition,
and has never been previously published.

BORDER DISPUTE

An Ace Book/published by arrangement with
the author

PRINTING HISTORY
Ace edition/April 1994

All rights reserved.
Copyright © 1994 by Jacqueline Lichtenberg.
Cover art by Cliff Miller.
This book may not be reproduced in whole or in part,
by mimeograph or any other means, without permission.
For information address: The Berkley Publishing Group,
200 Madison Avenue, New York, NY 10016.

ISBN: 0-441-00033-9

ACE®
Ace Books are published by The Berkley Publishing Group,
200 Madison Avenue, New York, NY 10016.
ACE and the "A" design are trademarks
belonging to Charter Communications, Inc.

PRINTED IN THE UNITED STATES OF AMERICA

10 9 8 7 6 5 4 3 2 1

This novel is dedicated to the men and women of the armed forces who put their lives on the line to defend our nation. No attempt has been made here to evoke the reality of such service, but neither did I intend to be irreverent, especially not of the women.

ACKNOWLEDGMENTS

As any author, I have had to draw upon the resources of entire networks of informants and critics. Here I must thank Quill and Screen Services for inspiration and information, the Klein family for producing a staunch ally and best friend, the U.S. Air Force for doing their job so well (a lot better than the First Tier Alliance, anyway!), Yonkers School District for exploring alternative command structures, and Brian Phillips for hours of painstaking proofreading.

In addition to those who contributed to the creation of this work, there are those who have labored to bring it forth onto the bookstands: Richard Curtis, my agent, who has had such faith in my product; Susan Allison, and the veritable army of professionals at Ace Books who do their jobs at least as well as the Air Force—and a lot better than the First Tier Alliance does theirs; and don't forget IBM and Microsoft, providers of the writer's miracle, the word processor!

★
CHAPTER
ONE
★

PILOT COMMANDER INDIW, FIRST TIER DEFENSE FORCE, Space Service, Retired, searched the canopy of stars arching over his land.

To his battle-trained perceptions, the star pattern revealed the nearby border between Hyos space and First Tier territories. Most suns of habitable planets were too dim to be perceptible to the naked eye, but he knew where they were. Mentally, he connected them with imaginary lines representing the well-traveled spacelanes, a random cross-hatched pattern.

He strained to imagine how such a random spattering of stars might look to a human. The latest text he'd smuggled onto Sinaha had shown a sketch of Earth's sky with lines connecting some brighter stars into figures of mythical gods, heroes, and animals, the symbolic components of the ferocious human psyche.

Each human culture had star pictures, and stories made from those pictures. The cultures that had won the most wars, exterminated the most lone-hunter animal species, had carried their myths into space, into Ardr territory.

Indiw let his eyes unfocus. Suddenly the stars outlined the figure of an Ardr gutting a human with his toe claws. He blinked and the image dissolved.

He suppressed a shudder of revulsion that his mind had

1

played such a trick—even though he'd invited the perception. He knew the image was inside him, not in the sky. The ancient humans had not known any such thing. They had created images that just weren't there, and then believed the images were real. But those images were the key to the real nature of the human threat for they came from deep inside the human psyche.

How could nature produce a species that appeared so very much like Ardr, yet functioned so very differently? True, humans lacked horns on their heads, and some older males cleaned the hair off as if to emphasize their deformity. Their skin was soft, moist, and no amount of polishing could make it shine. And it came in the most alarming array of colors. They could hardly smell, though their eyesight was keen enough in their own lighting. They had no real claws, either on hands or feet. But other than such minor differences, they were enough like Ardr to wear the same clothes if not sit comfortably in the same chairs.

Individually, they seemed puny, defenseless. Yet collectively, they were the most formidable threat Ardr had ever faced. Four years ago, Indiw, himself, had convinced a vast number of Ardr that humans were in fact no threat. Yet now that he understood more of them, he suspected he'd been wrong. He vanquished the disturbing thoughts, and stood up.

If his neighbors had any notion of what he was thinking, it could precipitate the last war humans or maybe Ardr might fight. Or, it might simply get him ostracized. He'd had enough of that four years ago when he'd flown combat missions with the humans. Even now, he hadn't lived the stigma down.

He stood atop the tumble of artfully piled boulders overlooking his favorite waterfall and surveyed his land. It was a large tract, fully two days hike across and four days hike long. At one point, he had his own private gate into the Walkway, open land where the females waited to choose partners for this balmy spring evening. And he had become a very popular partner among them.

As the wind shifted, his horns tingled with the faint

female scent wafting across the lush greenery. Indiw's heart raced. For the twentieth time in four years, he vowed never again to risk smuggling human writings onto Sinaha. But this time, he meant it. Life was just too good to risk.

Now he planned to take full advantage of that goodness. From horn tips to claw tips, his whole body knew how to get the most out of the high regard of his female neighbors.

Awash in anticipation, he knelt, eased over the edge of the boulder to hang-drop down to the next ledge.

The night sky flashed dazzling white, then iridescent.

Indiw dropped and rolled under an overhang. He hunkered in the meager shelter, eyes closed against the lethal glare. His heart pounded again, but with a different excitement.

The light had been from a Hyos sonic bomb detonated in close orbit by hitting a First Tier single-seat fighter. The smeared iridescence was unmistakable.

Screening his eyes with both hands, Indiw dared survey the darkening sky for fast-moving sparks among the stars and planets. Infinitesimal specks of light flashed and died against the pristine dark. Fighters, Hyos and Tier, dying in a desperate fight for possession of the planet.

It had been two years since battle had come this close to Sinaha. Back then he had not been a land holder.

He half stood, peering up over the ledge above him, back toward the saw-toothed horizon where the new, experimental cannon had been installed on Tantigre Peak, the highest mountain in this hemisphere. It was just a prototype, but it was on-line and ready for testing. Why wasn't it firing?

A green streak arced from horizon to horizon, an empty Hyos tanker hitting the outer planetary defenses. Before the light died, the entire bowl of sky turned bright red. Indiw had only seen that before in drills. It was the close-in defense shield. The new cannon couldn't fire through that.

But he was a fighter pilot. He knew how little the shield would be worth in the end. He also knew better than to look directly at it with the naked eye.

Head down, he scrambled to the ground and ran for his house. He had to find out what was going on.

Three times he flung himself prone, burrowing with hand and toe claws for cover against the bursts of ultraviolet from destroyed craft. As he reached his front door, the sky brightened unbearably into a scintillating daytime blue as if a new sun had been born in close orbit.

And for just that one moment, it had.

Worse, the defense shield had failed, or the color would have been purple, not blue. Indiw plunged inside and barked orders to the house system, bringing up every information service he had. Half of them responded.

He found the strategic tracking data he needed on the tactical databoard. It had cost him a fortune to subscribe, but now it took only moments to gain the whole picture.

The small sun that had burst and died in close orbit had been *Katular,* the Ardr carrier posted to protect this border from Hyos incursion. With it gone, there was nothing between Sinaha and the encroaching Hyos swarm except the few deployed *Katular* fighters and the tattered planetary defenses.

Already he could feel the deep vibration of the planet-based launchers flinging out scatter shot of orbital mines designed to make descent lethal. It would do little good. The Hyos had sweepers to clear their way, as did the Ardr fighters remaining in orbit.

And there was no sign of the new weapon.

So, this is how it will end. After two years of being landed, he would die in defense of his land. There was no better way to die, but it was too soon. After all the years of striving, he'd only just tasted the good life.

Most of his neighbors would feel the same way, for they, too, had just retired from combat posts. The Hyos wouldn't take this valley without destroying its fertility and beauty first. The battle of Sinaha wouldn't end when the First Tier government declared Sinaha lost. The treaty with the Hyos stipulated that every landed Ardr would defend the land to the death. It was pure instinct. Hyos understood instinct.

Unaware of the snarl on his lips, Indiw hit the control plate at the rear edge of his desk. All around his land, defenses rose, subtle traps for the unwary. Most were designed to trick an Ardr invader intent on gaining land by personal combat. But he'd also invested heavily in items geared to Hyos invaders, even Hyos in battle armor.

Once, on *Tacoma,* he'd faced a phalanx of armored Hyos intent on taking the ship. Here, he had no chance against such a force, but his strip of land wouldn't attract so much attention. He could do serious damage before they got him.

He grabbed a few essentials, set everything on automatic or remote control, and locked his boards down with his personal security code—Pit Bull—a code no Ardr, and certainly no Hyos, would ever guess. Even a direct hit on this control center would not disarm his defense system.

He paused at the hidden door to his basement, hand hovering over one last control plate. Teeth clenched over wrenching emotion, he struck the switch.

All over the house, scent eradicator sprayed from hidden atomizers, the mist settling over every surface. With that one act, he had ceded his very home to the hands of invaders. He knew it wasn't necessary. Hyos would never notice scent markings. But he also knew he'd never be able to blow the place up, even to kill the Hyos inside, if he still regarded it as *home*. Now it was just a building.

In the basement, he approached the camouflaged door down into the cave system underlying his land, spraying eradicator behind him until he sneezed. He sealed the door behind himself. Now no invader could find this access point.

Fifteen minutes later, panting with exertion, Indiw emerged at the top of a rise that commanded the more fertile half of his land. Here, he had built a redoubt over a natural water supply and stocked it with food and every weapon legal on planetary surfaces.

It was energy-shielded to be undetectable from space. Visually it blended into the hilltop. Any attacker would go first to the house, thinking to claim the nerve center of the defenses. But from this hilltop retreat, Indiw could monitor his house and dispose of the intruder or the whole house.

He had had plans to add two more such command centers

at the farthest points of his land. He had had so many plans.

He sat at the control console and summoned his master defense systems. Everything responded except his taps into the public systems. Even the tactical databoard was black.

His own meager instruments showed the new cannon on Tantigre Peak fire a white ball of energy that expanded as it rose through the atmosphere. Moments later six helpless fighters descended leaving meteoric streaks behind them.

Then all planetary power grids went down. Something major had been hit. The cannon didn't have an independent power feed yet. Without the grids, the cannon was gone.

All of his viewscreens now showed black sky. An eerie silence spread over the land. He waited, but nothing happened. He didn't have enough sensors around his perimeter to get an accurate picture. Eventually, he climbed out of his uppermost turret to search the sky with his own eyes.

There was nothing. Just stars.

So it's over and we lost. Now it begins.

The moment the thought formed, a solitary yellow streak arced across his vision, a fighter burning up in atmosphere. It came down steeply, checked, redirected, faltered as if the pilot fought a monumental battle against failing systems, and then plunged to the ground sending up an immense fireball. Immediately, the thunder deafened him.

That was close! It must have come down in his swamp where he usually hunted. What if the pilot had survived? It didn't matter if it were Hyos or Ardr, there was no way the intruder would walk Indiw's land. No way.

He sealed the redoubt, taking only his weapons and his remotes. He had to dodge his own traps, so it took nearly twenty minutes to get to the crest of the ridge overlooking the swamp. A charred furrow arrowed across the low shrubs. At its far end, the soft-trunked trees of the swamp lay like kindling sticks, all pointed away from the metallic lump that was the pilot's ejection capsule, still sealed.

The brittle winter grasses had gone up in flame, and now they were nothing but ash. Everything else was too wet to burn, except one lone tree that stood like a torch, flames shooting to the sky. Way off to his right, Indiw could see the spot where the main body of the fighter had crashed and exploded. Around it, heavy vegetation burned sullenly, thick smoke blowing away from him.

He scrambled down into the swamp and waded across, zigzagging to follow the ridges where the water was shallow. He had to travel by smell, for the night had turned pitch-dark. Beyond the light of the burning tree, he couldn't see well enough to identify the vegetation. But he didn't slacken pace. He would not allow the intruder out of that capsule.

His toe claws ached with anticipation. The last time he'd disemboweled a Hyos, he'd been fighting beside Walter Falstaff, defending the carrier *Tacoma*. He hadn't gutted another Ardr since he'd been a child, but he well remembered the intense satisfaction of it. And, since he was now landed, it was once again legal for him to kill.

He approached the capsule with his long knife glowing in one hand and his electronic lock-pick in the other. Hyos or Ardr, he'd have that capsule open in just. . . .

By the light of the burning tree, the symbol etched into the skin of the bullet-shaped capsule was clear even though all the paint had been scorched off. *Tacoma*.

The pilot was human.

If the pilot was also female. . . . Indiw refused to think about that. In his experience, human females were the worst enemies. It would have to be a quick, clean kill.

He reset his lock-pick for human protocols and the canopy slid back with a screech of buckled metal.

Choking, acrid smoke billowed out. Indiw holstered his knife and scooped fetid water into the cockpit to kill the fire. Then, claws ready, he leaned across the cowling to do what had to be done. The instrument panel gave one last sparkling flash. By that light, he saw the helmet roll toward him and he struck reflexively at the intruder.

It was a stupid reflex. His claws slashed toward the pilot's throat and snagged in the tough flight suit.

With two claws caught in the neck seal, he saw the name blazoned across the front of the helmet. Raymond

G. Falstaff, Jr., Pilot Lieutenant, *Tacoma.*

His claws bit into the fabric, and he pulled the head around, but the visor was opaque with soot and the darkness within. The head lolled to one side. Dead?

With a savage twist, Indiw yanked the helmet off.

The naked face was pale except where blood crusted below the nose and still flowed freely. But there was no mistaking it. It was Walter G. Falstaff's face. Falstaff had been the best pilot Indiw had ever known.

Raymond Falstaff was his nephew, the son of his brother. But he didn't look like another person. He looked like the same person, only younger.

With a sudden, inexplicable horror, Indiw dropped the limp form back into the cockpit and pushed away from the capsule. The burning tree cast a flickering, eerie light that made it seem his friend, his drinking buddy, his flying partner, was lying there bleeding.

But he'd died four years ago. He'd died when a Hyos had sliced his torso across. He'd died defending this—child— and the planet Aberdeen from the Hyos. He was dead. He was gone. Yet here he was—dying again.

Indiw twisted away, torn by instinct in conflict with memories. Emotions washed through him in riptides stirring things best left alone by the civilized.

When it was over, he was limp, shaking, and sick with the knowledge that—no matter what—he couldn't gut this intruder. He *could not.*

So what could he do? Leave him here to die? The night wind and plummeting temperature would produce a frozen corpse. Then the neighbors wouldn't discover his aberration.

He turned to go, hacking at charred brush with his knife.

The human moaned.

It was Walter Falstaff's voice.

Indiw froze. The sound didn't come again, but his feet would not carry him away.

Afterward, he had no idea how long he'd stood, muscle locked against muscle, instinct short-circuited in painful sparks that seared his innermost psyche.

Then he turned back to the capsule and took the first small step that would lock him into the fate he'd avoided when he'd survived the battle of Aberdeen, where the earlier *Tacoma* had taken so much damage it had to be scrapped.

Head down, body tense, jaws locked, he heaved the limp form out of the capsule, slung it over his shoulders, and slogged back toward his house.

He couldn't take an intruder to his redoubt. The house would have to do. After all, he'd ceded it to invaders. He could only hope that *Tacoma* had arrived in time, that *Tacoma* had won, and no Hyos would come to destroy the house.

And then all coherent thought was set aside. It took all his energy to cut trail through the active defenses, in the dark, the cold, carrying a burden massing as much as he did. Twice, he fell, once dumping the human into the thick ooze of a gully cut by the last rain. That made it much harder to grip the mud-slicked flight suit. He was tempted to stop and peel it off, but exposure to these temperatures would surely kill a human.

By the time he reached the house, he had it all planned. As soon as the human was conscious, he'd swear him to secrecy and let him steal the aircar. Falstaff could say he'd crashed, hiked toward some lights, and had stolen the car knowing the owner of the land would kill him if he could. It was perfectly logical. Doubtless, it was what the human would have done. No pilot flew Ardr skies without knowing the penalty for an injudicious landing.

On the back porch, Indiw laid his burden down and extracted the soft-fleshed human—sweating and stinking—from his flight suit. The discarded casing smelled even worse than the human.

He wrapped him in a ground tarp from the garden and left him there. He went around to the exterior control box, disarmed the house defenses, entered by the front door, carefully leaving the scent post untouched, and went through to the back sleeping quarters that opened onto the porch.

The body was just as he'd left it. He hefted the limp

form, staggered into the house, turned up the heat, and rolled the damp, reeking human into his nice, clean sand bed.

The fine white sand stuck to the human's skin. He should have spread fabric over the sand. He'd been studying the human mind so minutely, he'd forgotten about the body.

Amid his camping supplies, he found ground cloths and spread one under the body, another over it to protect the human skin from the sap. It was an expensive variety of healing tree, but would do the human no good.

He brought basins of warm water, stripped the human bare, and washed him down, searching for injuries. The nose stopped bleeding as he cleaned the blood away.

The upper lip was distorted, swollen, but not broken, and the formidable front teeth seemed undamaged. Once the blood matting the hair was removed, he saw the skull had not taken any serious damage, though there was a nasty bruise over one eye. At least the boy kept his head hair almost as short as he kept the hair patches on the rest of his body.

Indiw found some mild redness on the soft skin as if from burns, but no serious radiation damage. By the time he finished, the human still had not regained consciousness. Why? Then he remembered to check the eyes. It seemed that one pupil just might be slightly less light sensitive than the other.

In a human, that could be serious. But maybe not.

To his chagrin, a part of him yearned for the invader to die and leave him in peace.

Then he wondered if this Falstaff had reproduced yet. Was he too young? Or was there another copy of Walter Falstaff in pilot's training somewhere? Would he be haunted by Falstaffs all his life if he didn't save this one?

If this young Falstaff did not regain consciousness soon, he would have to fly him to the public field himself so *Tacoma*'s medics could pick him up—and everyone would know what he'd done. Even if he said he'd found the human on public land, they would know. Ardr could smell a lie.

He brought layers of warm, dry coverings and turned the heat in the room up. Then he went to improvise something hot he could feed the boy. As he worked through the labels on everything in his larder, he monitored the one information net that had come back on-line.

Tacoma had arrived just in time to vanquish the Hyos swarm, but Sinaha had taken major damage to power services and defense installations, including the new cannon. Three permanent satellites had been hit. One public training center for young, unlanded Ardr was nothing but a five-mile-wide smoking hole in the ground. The Hyos always went for population concentrations, thinking they'd be more important than the scattered holdings. Strange prejudice.

For the moment, the immediate threat had abated and nothing had been lost that couldn't easily be replaced.

Carrying a bowl of hot soup made from an odd concatenation of vegetables, Indiw returned to his patient. It was almost dawn. The wind had picked up, rushing through the surrounding forest, rolling banks of clouds up from the horizon. The weather display showed a pelting rain would fall all day, an icy rain. It would have been a lovely day for a run, if only he'd spent the evening as he'd planned.

He settled beside the sand bed, bleakly contemplating his future. If ever it became known what he'd done, he'd never again be chosen by any female. And he was much too young to regard that with equanimity.

He reached out a hand, claws hard retracted, and tilted the human face toward him. "Well, Raymond G. Falstaff, Jr., don't you think it's about time you woke up?"

A split instant later he faced a bristling human crouched to spring at him with lethal intent.

Indiw kicked his chair back and, claws out, braced to meet that spring.

But it never came.

The mobile human countenance flickered through several expressions. Indiw knew the human could barely see in the normal indoor lighting, and even pure sunlight would not help much, especially on a dark day like this.

Squinting, the human straightened and assumed the best

human imitation of a nonthreatening stance. "Indiw? Are you Pilot Commander Indiw?"

Indiw recoiled. Most humans had a very hard time telling Ardr apart, and Indiw bore no distinguishing scars. In this light, the human should not be able to identify him.

"I'm Walter Falstaff's nephew," offered the human.

"I know," said Indiw. "I saw you on a news clip four years ago, claiming you wanted to be a hero like your uncle."

"You saw that? Oh, shit. I was such a stupid kid."

"Are you an adult now?"

The stance stiffened to an offended dignity. "Yes."

"Are you still stupid?" *What if he has reproduced?*

"What!?" As if the starch had all suddenly washed out of him, the naked human sank to his knees on the cloth-covered sand. One hand went to his head and he doubled over. "Well, I guess so. I got burned by the clumsiest Hyos in creation. But I nailed him before I hit atmosphere."

"And came down on private land."

The human face raised, a pale oval backlit by the hazy dawn. "But you *are* Indiw, aren't you?"

"And how would you know?"

"This's your land, isn't it? That's what the map said."

"You *chose* to come down on *my* land!"

"We lost *Katular* to the Hyos. I lost my wingman today, and I'll bet it's not over yet. The swarms are cooperating with each other, more now than four years ago. It has to be the first move in a new assault on the border. I didn't know any other way to convince you to come back and fly with Pit Bull—than face-to-face. And I knew you'd never *let* me come talk to you! So when I got hit, I nursed my engines along so I'd land here. I *knew* you wouldn't kill me, not if you knew who I was. I didn't plan on getting knocked out."

He *knew*?! No. The human simply didn't understand. If it hadn't been for the flight suit protecting against Indiw's claws, he'd have been dead.

"And you didn't kill me!" Falstaff said brightly. "You saved my life."

Dumbfounded, Indiw gaped at the confused child.

"So what do you say? Re-up and fly with Pit Bull. Give the Hyos hell! Come on, I gotta call in and you can tell Captain—"

Abruptly Indiw turned away, and the human fell silent.

The boy had sounded just like Walter Falstaff. It was more than having the same brown eyes, and brown hair, or the same pale skin and sharp features. It was the way he held himself, the way he ignited at the prospect of action.

But Indiw also had noted how the eyes glittered feverishly, how the skin around the cracked lips was too pale in contrast to the bruises and pink swellings. And the voice strained with suppressed pain. This was not a well human.

He turned back. "You're in no condition to give anyone hell but yourself. I'll get you a robe and food. When you are rested, I'll give you my car. You can go to the public field where *Tacoma* can pick you up. Nothing need be said to anyone about this. You understand?"

"Oh, Commander Indiw, I wouldn't embarrass you in front of your neighbors! My uncle wouldn't have, would he?"

Indiw made him pull the robe on, a simple broadly cut garment designed to confine the body's scents when it would be impolite to broadcast one's arousal. Falstaff had worn one like it aboard *Katular*. It emphasized the resemblance.

He didn't want to think about this Falstaff's words. "Here," he said, proffering the soup. "This is all I have fit for human nourishment. Then you must sleep before you can leave." *And then I will cleanse your scent out of my house!*

The human took the bowl. It was still warm, and he inhaled the aroma. It seemed acceptable, though Indiw wouldn't have touched the concoction. Eagerly, he tilted the bowl up to sip at the warm liquid.

His enthusiasm for the soup waned abruptly. He shoved the bowl at Indiw, dropping it in midair before Ardr claws could close around it. One hand over his mouth, he muttered, "I think I'm going to—I'm going to—be sick." Then he was jackknifed over the edge of the sand bed heaving his insides out. Fortunately, he'd drunk very little of the soup and produced barely a trickle of bile.

Weak and drained, he flopped back onto the sand panting. "I'm sorry! I'll clean it up—just a mo—"

"No! Don't move. Such things happen after head injuries. It is of no consequence. You must remain still and without moving. You must sleep." *But what if it is serious? What if it gets worse?*

Yet the human's eyes seemed to be the same size now. Or was that wishful thinking? The disparity had never been very great. And after all, the boy was conscious now.

Even as Indiw pondered this, the human's head lolled to one side as if much too heavy for him to manage. He muttered, " . . . contact *Tacoma* . . . tell them I'm on my . . ." Before he could finish the utterance, he fell asleep with his mouth open. It seemed a natural sleep.

Indiw remembered how Falstaff's first concern when he'd wakened on *Katular* had been to report to his unit so he wouldn't be penalized. Indiw hadn't understood then, but now he knew how a human joining a pack bound himself to obey nonsensical strictures—which they nevertheless took very seriously.

Then he savagely squelched the thought. He didn't want to know, he didn't want to understand. He only wanted to get rid of the human as quickly and quietly as possible.

He cleaned up the room with liberal amounts of scent eradicator. Then he tended to the ravages the night's activities had taken on his own hide. He was covered with layers of mud, soot, and pond scum laced with the sticky sap of various night-bloomers. He reeked worse than the human.

Once clean, he buffed his torso until it gleamed, sharpened his horns, and donned his best sandals and insignia straps tinted the exact shade of the two small but perfectly curved horns that graced his skull, the best straps his newly landed status allowed. He cut an imposing figure.

He completed his grooming just in time. Around noon, the message service came back on-line dropping five messages into his buffer.

Three were from neighbors who'd noticed the fireball come down on his land—checking up, no doubt, to see if he'd survived or if they had a chance to annex his property. He dropped terse notes just to indicate his land was still held. Firmly held. Then he tended to the official queries.

In the aftermath of battle, tracking stations strove to locate the crashed fighters, hostiles as well as defenders. Those who had managed to crash on public lands or waters had already been picked up by Search and Rescue from *Tacoma*, but by treaty, the humans could not chase their lost fighters onto held land.

As Indiw pondered what to say about the fighter they probably knew had crashed in his swamp, the comweb burped, flashed, and produced a distraught human's face over a bit of uniform with a fighter wing captain's insignia.

"—don't care if you have to—oh! Excuse me, do I have the honor of addressing the land holder Indiw? Pilot Commander Indiw, Retired?"

The connection should not have been made without his activating his own board. He had a bad circuit. Indiw aborted his impulse to slam down the disconnect.

"Honored Land Holder, I am Wing Captain Jules Lorton. I do apologize for the intrusion. We've lost a fighter on your land and would appreciate the return of his recorder—and whatever may remain of the pilot, Lieutenant Raymond G. Falstaff, Jr." The human swallowed hugely, causing the bump in his neck to bob up and down.

He has made this request several times already, to other land holders who have dispatched their trespassers and returned the gutted corpses. "I will keep your preference in mind," Indiw answered and moved to cut the connection.

"Please, wait! Falstaff was the last survivor of Pit Bull Squadron. We could surely use your help. We've lost a lot—" He turned away as something off screen attracted his attention, and Indiw caught a distant voice.

"—another wave of Hyos incoming, thirty degrees above the ecliptic. We've too many fighters down now. Get the Ardr to scramble anything that can make it into space and defend their own bloody planet."

A faint odor reached Indiw's nostrils, too faint to register on his horns. Human. He turned aghast as Falstaff reeled right into Captain Lorton's line of sight. "Pilot Falstaff reporting for duty, sir! I'll be at the public field in twenty minutes for pickup. But my fighter's totaled, and my wingman here hasn't got a rivet to his name!"

Rivet? What could that be? The inane question filled the void left in Indiw's mind by shock.

Lorton's gaze flicked from Falstaff to Indiw and back, then his tired face lit with a grin, fierce teeth hanging out in challenge. Indiw recoiled involuntarily, but Lorton didn't notice. "Report to Hangar C in one hour, Lieutenant. Commander Indiw, welcome aboard and welcome to Delta Wing. Your commission reactivation will be waiting. Now, if you'll excuse me, I have to marshal our forces."

The screen went black.

Indiw, paralyzed by shock, barely heard Falstaff's hearty, "Congratulations, Commander, and welcome aboard. And thank you for calling in before they socked me with a fine. I was real worried how I was going to explain surviving on private land without giving you away! Let's go!"

CHAPTER TWO

★

INDIW, NUMBED TO HIS VERY CORE BY THE BIZARRE twist his fate had taken, nevertheless knew he'd had no choice but to fly. Any land holder would use any skill he had to defend his land. Indiw was a fighter pilot, one of the very best. When Lorton had broadcast his appeal across Sinaha for every available Ardr pilot, Indiw would have responded as all others did, would have flown whatever would make orbit, and would have joined with any flight grouping to fight Hyos.

And that is exactly what the other retired pilots on Sinaha had done. En masse, they had reported to *Tacoma*'s landing bay to take anything they knew how to fly in combat.

However, Indiw, arriving in a commercial shuttle along with Falstaff, two other human pilots, and twenty-six Ardr combat pilots, had been greeted by the humans of *Tacoma* not as an Ardr but as one of their own. They had presented him with a flight suit complete with Commander insignia and swept him into a fighter painted with the Pit Bull logo.

Before he knew what was happening, he was lined up in the launch chute behind Falstaff and a Squadron Commander Witter of the Hawk Squadron whose wingman was the last of Wild Blue Squadron.

Indiw had no choice but to fly the formation—in full view of three hundred Ardr pilots grouping to attack the incoming Hyos. If, at that point, he'd gone to weave pattern with the Ardr, the Ardr would have excluded him.

There was no doubt in his mind that by the time he returned to the ground, word would be out that he'd failed to kill the human intruder on his land. He no longer had any future on Sinaha. But done was done.

However it had happened, done was done. He had been too shocked to speak in the aircar. He hadn't dared to exchange even one word with Falstaff on the shuttle—not in full view of so many Ardr. But by then it was too late. It had been too late from the moment Lorton had spotted Raymond G. Falstaff, Jr., in Indiw's house. On *Tacoma*, anything he said to Lorton would have been in full hearing of a dozen Ardr who were already shrinking from him.

The boy had made a natural mistake—for a human. But it had probably shortened Indiw's life expectancy.

He could not afford to think about it now. There was a mission to fly. He squirmed uncomfortably in his human-tailored flight suit, then ran his instrument checks. At least his throttled kill instinct would soon be assuaged.

He was expert with every design quirk of the new instrumentation. He had, after all, been the designer. It had earned him his land. He'd figured a way to circuit the boards so the instrument readings weren't as vulnerable to radiation. That incidentally increased their sensitivity, range, speed, and accuracy by reducing circuit path.

He grinned ferociously when the vivid new tactical display lit to show some five hundred Hyos fighters approaching Sinaha—not a full swarm.

They were probably the survivors of some defeated swarm with nowhere to go and no hope left. That would make them a formidable threat. The advance edge of *Tacoma*'s tattered fighter wings engaged the enemy while Indiw waited launch.

The Hyos fought like demons, ramming their craft into the defenders when they were out of fuel or ammunition. Falstaff had been right, Hyos tactics had changed over the last couple of years, after decades of unvarying behavior.

As he studied the Hyos movements looking for other innovations, Witter's voice—which had been droning in the background—penetrated. "Okay, Pit Bull Three and Pit Bull Four, it's agreed. We are now Splinter Squadron. And you know where that splinter's gonna go—the one place on a Hyos where the sun don't shine! Let's stick it to 'em, guys."

A ragged cheer went up as the launchers spewed them out into space. "Close up, Splinter Four! That's you, Commander Indiw! Get right up close to Falstaff there. Good! Let's go get 'em."

Indiw didn't have his own subroutines programmed into this fighter's memory. He hadn't thought to grab his modules at home—they were installed in his simulator, the only way he'd flown in the last two years. Now, as he watched the glittering wall of battle approach, his guilty sessions with the human-style squadron simulation came back full force. He had told himself he flew human style to try to get into their minds enough to understand their books. But the real reason, he could admit now, was that he *liked* it.

"Splinter Four, this is Splinter Three," came Falstaff's voice on their private band. "Stick on my tail now 'cause here we go. And, Commander, whatever they say, you and I *are* Pit Bull! We're just flying with Splinter right now. So let's show them what we can do." Falstaff didn't sound weak or sick now.

Indiw stole a moment from programming his fighter's memory to return a terse "Acknowledged, Lieutenant Falstaff." It never occurred to him that using Falstaff's rank in that context had been a subtle put-down that erroneously led the young human to assume Indiw had a firm grasp of human command protocols.

He was too busy noting how the Ardr contingent had taken responsibility for the enemy's left-hand flank. They had already carved a chunk out of the main Hyos body and were isolating it to be devoured piecemeal.

Then Splinter was chasing a Hyos. Witter got that one. A Hyos missile hit Witter and his shields whited out, but when the dazzle cleared, he was in one piece. His wingman

got the culprit with a slicer, and Falstaff took off after a
Hyos who nearly drilled Witter's wingman.

Indiw stuck with Falstaff, watching his tail. A Hyos spun
toward them fleeing the Ardr pattern that was englobing
their prey. The singleton leveled off heading for Falstaff.
Indiw broke formation and loosed two rapid cannon shots,
missed with the first and nailed the Hyos with the second.
The Hyos broke apart. As Indiw streaked through the spot
where the Hyos had been, his shields repelled debris.

"Great flying, Indiw—shit, man, *dive!*"

Indiw nosed below the plane of reference and a red
beam flashed through the space he'd occupied. He did
a one-eighty, looping above the plane of reference, and
found Falstaff screaming for help as he pounded away at
a Hyos craft that was larger than the others.

At first, Indiw didn't understand what he was seeing.
This larger craft fired energy beams simultaneously in four
directions. It must have four autonomous targeting comput-
ers. How could a pilot handle four—no! There were four
Hyos on that one craft—a pilot and three gunners.

Now *that* was a change.

Indiw loosed a barrage of missiles at the monstrous
thing, following them in to pound away with his cannon.
He took two direct hits—the craft had no blind spot—and
streaked past. By the time he circled back, Witter and his
wingman had joined Falstaff, firing their cannons.

But they were making no progress. Indiw stood back
from the fight and ran a quick digital image of the monster,
looking for a weak spot.

"Splinter One, this is Splinter Four. The only vulnerable
spot in this thing's shield is the cannon ports. The shields
fade right over the port before it fires."

"We know," answered Witter. "We can kill these only
by overwhelming their shields with cannon fire."

"I can hit the port, sir."

"Nobody can shoot that well. We'll get some help here
in a couple of minutes."

With his right hand, Indiw taught his computer a timed
sequence he'd often used with the simulator. With his left

hand he maneuvered away for a long run at the monster. His innovations had increased the computer's speed but he hadn't been able to convince anybody to take full advantage of that yet. Now he'd show them.

"Cover me," he suggested, "and we'll see if we really need help. Here I come. Port side cannon."

He began his run before the others agreed. But Falstaff fell in before him as if they'd practiced this a dozen times. Falstaff set his shields to overlap Indiw's, his slicers raking the target to confuse their sensors. At the last moment, Falstaff peeled off to the right, drawing fire, and Indiw bored in on his target.

His instruments pegged the instant the Hyos cannon port opened as the weapon targeted Falstaff. Indiw held his course, and his little program did the rest.

His cannon delivered a glowing ball of energy, then he sheared away into a steep climb. Behind him, a blue ball of light expanded. The energy wave bounced off his shields.

"Got him! Hot damn, Indiw, you're one helluva pilot!" That was Witter's wingman. Indiw didn't know his name.

Falstaff yelled, "Watch your tail, Indiw."

Something hit Indiw and spun him out of control. Then everything whited out. When it cleared and he regained control, the battle was over and Falstaff was pleading, "You okay, man? Splinter Four, come on, talk to me!"

"This is Splinter Four. All systems functional, but guidance is on backup."

"You had me worried! Splinter One, this is Splinter Three. Four and I are okay, but Indiw's on backup guidance."

"Good work, guys. Form on me. *Tacoma* says it's all over and we're to come home. We've taken the least damage, so we'll bring up the rear. Falstaff, the two of you fly like you've been together for years. Never seen anything like it."

"We're Pit Bull Squadron," answered Falstaff smugly.

As they formed for the flight back to *Tacoma*, Indiw noted the holes in the other squadrons. Even in this brief fight, they'd taken heavy damage. And, as they approached their landing bay, he noted several new scars on *Tacoma*'s gleaming hide. With the fighting wings below full strength, several of those monstrous gunships had gotten through. That was probably how *Katular* had been destroyed. He wondered if any of the monsters had made it into atmosphere and what kind of planetary weapons such a ship might carry.

In the landing bay, as soon as the mechanics pried open his canopy, Indiw fumbled his light-translating visor into place and levered himself out of the cockpit. Not looking right or left, he made for the nearest lift.

Unlike his first time among humans, he knew if he could contact the Quartermaster's office, he would find out where they'd assigned him quarters. Once he had his Orders nodule, he knew he could get everything he needed on the ship. There was a chance he could do all that before they called their Interview. A dim memory reminded him they called that process debriefing. *Idiot word—as if the pilots unlearned everything that happened by telling about it!*

Walking in a fog, he found himself at the lift at which Falstaff waited, helmet tucked under one arm, a cockeyed grin on his face. But he covered his teeth as Indiw approached.

Indiw shied away from the human, expecting exuberance expressed the same way as the elder Falstaff's, with a blow of the open hand. Such a blow from an Ardr would rake killing claws through flesh to the bone. But this Falstaff tucked his free hand behind him and tilted forward in friendly salutation.

The human's brown eyes glowed with overflowing good spirits. "We really did give 'em hell! You're better than any of the records of your battles showed! You gotta teach me how you did that trick with the fire control computer. You've got to teach me everything!"

"I don't know if I'll be around that long." He stepped into the lift and to his discomfort Falstaff followed.

"Don't say that. Hyos'll never get you, Commander."

"I meant that I intend to resign and go home." There was nothing to be gained by avoiding the consequences of his decision to spare this young human's life. "I never intended to rejoin Pit Bull Squadron."

Falstaff's face fell into tense, vertical lines.

"You misunderstood, Lieutenant. Captain Lorton called me, not I him. I had not told him that you had survived. I had not intended to. I flew this mission only to protect my land. It's over. As soon as I inform the Records Officer of my resignation, I will be gone."

The pale human turned paler. "You mean I—I blew it for you! Oh, God, Indiw—Commander—I didn't mean—I'd never have—you have to believe me—"

"It was an honest mistake such as any human might make. I will accept your mistakes if you will accept mine. This should be my deck. Excuse me."

The doors flicked open revealing a long, gleaming corridor lined with open hatches and permeated with the muted sounds of office equipment. Throngs of humans flowed to and fro. Dressed in all varieties of ship's uniform save that of pilot, they were all intent on their own business.

Indiw stepped into the press, thinking to escape Falstaff once and for all. But the human followed him. He danced along in an awkward sideways gait as Indiw strode toward the larger offices at the end of the corridor where the Quartermaster and the Records Officer were located.

"Commander Indiw, don't cut me off. Please. Give me a chance. Let me make it right. I never meant to get you into any trouble. You have to believe that."

Indiw stopped and traffic continued to stream around them, faces turning as they noticed his Ardr features. Some frowned, but most smiled their best (and most ferocious) welcoming smiles. "Lieutenant Falstaff, I do believe your innocent intent. And *that* is why I wish to place myself as far away from you as possible."

Indiw had had no idea that the human countenance could express such thunderstruck devastation. He was so enthralled by the unexpected silent eloquence—possibly a compensation for the human olfactory impairment—that he almost missed its significance. Excruciating pain.

As Falstaff began to turn away, shoulders slumped, Indiw snapped, "I apologize! Now I have made one of those mistakes that any Ardr might make. I did not intend to express any opinion of you, personally. I intended only to express my choice clearly. It has nothing to do with you, your actions, or your ability to fly, but only with my personal choice."

"Choice? Oh. I see. I understand. My mistake. I thought you'd chosen to fly with Pit Bull again. I thought I'd have a chance to learn—well . . . Thank you, Commander. Thank you for saving my life. Thank you for flying with me. Thank you for nailing that Hyos that almost got me. I'll remember every moment of it for the rest of my life. Every moment. Good-bye."

Falstaff saluted, then executed a formal pivot and walked stiffly back to the lift. Indiw watched him go, wondering why he sensed the human emitting throbbing waves of grief even through the mélange of odors in the corridor.

He throttled his curiosity and renewed his resolve to drop the study of humanity. Just look where it had gotten him. Resolute, he took himself into the Records Office, surveying the array of functionaries behind a counter. To one side, there was a short alley made by low partitions that surrounded desks. Each emplacement was identified by a small brass sign bearing cryptic abbreviations. He would have to ask for assistance.

Suddenly, there was an immense wall of uniform in front of his nose and a voice boomed, "Commander Indiw, welcome to *Tacoma*'s Delta Wing."

He retreated and tilted his head back. Atop the huge expanse of uniform was the face of Captain Lorton. The human stood with his open hand extended, exuding joy and goodwill.

Retracting his claws tightly, Indiw took the proffered hand, returning the pressure firmly, then releasing it. To his relief, Lorton let go immediately. Then the human stepped back and gave a little bow, perhaps meant as a polite greeting though the posture was all wrong.

"Thank you, Captain Lorton. But I must speak to you—"

They were interrupted by a yeoman who handed Lorton a flat case. "Here they are, Captain, everything you requested." He stepped aside, staring covertly at Indiw.

"Thank you, Yeoman. You may go."

"Sir!" The man retreated behind his counter.

Lorton passed the case to Indiw. "There you go, Commander. I think you'll find everything you need inside. With your Orders nodule, the Quartermaster can issue you all the gear you'll need. We'll be taking on Ardr supplies before we leave Sinaha, so I think you'll be—"

"Captain, I wanted to speak to you about—"

"Don't worry about a thing. I came down here personally to walk your orders through because I know how difficult this must be for you—and because we need you. That youngster—Falstaff?—I had no idea how right he was when he insisted we had to have you back flying again if we were to deal with those new porkies the Hyos have. But you proved him right today. You're the only one who really understands that new circuitry of yours and what it can do."

"Sir, I—"

"Don't be modest. In my wing, a man gets the credit he deserves—and the promotions with pay to match. Now, we have to master that innovation you showed us today. And fast. Check with my office in the morning. I'll have your teaching schedule set and a simulator cleared for your class. Your work will be recorded, of course, and sent to all the other carriers flying the new fighters. And I'll personally see that your three best students are sent to other carriers to teach. It might just turn the tide for us."

He started to move past Indiw.

Indiw tried again, "Captain Lorton, it won't work. I've been trying to tell—"

Lorton checked and held up both hands, palm out. "Falstaff told me how little luck you've had getting Ardr pilots to use the new instruments, but I couldn't believe Ardr pilots were so conservative until I saw your system in action. Like I said before, welcome aboard. And you can virtually write your own ticket here. We need everything you can

tell us about that new system of yours! But you're off duty
for the next sixteen hours. Get a good rest because we're
going to work you hard. Debriefing at oh-eight-hundred,
and your classes will start at ten-hundred sharp. It's all in
your orders."

Lorton turned away again and then added, "Oh, and tell
Falstaff he's going to get a commendation for this if I have
anything to say about it. Everyone ought to learn to read at
least one of the languages of another species."

Falstaff had been reading the Ardr journals? Before he
could digest that, Lorton was gone.

Indiw had published a number of articles about his circuitry design, trying to get pilots to experiment with it, but
his suggestions had been greeted with indifference.

Obviously, Lorton and maybe Falstaff thought that was
because Ardr pilots didn't want to change their methods.
But Ardr were still leery of the human taint they suspected Indiw carried. They accepted the hardware eagerly,
but would not touch any tactical by-product of his design
innovations.

If Indiw used this opportunity to teach humans the limits
of the new equipment and they based new tactics on the
new capabilities, it would confirm every Ardr's worst fear
about him. But if he didn't teach them and the Hyos over-
ran the border, the entire defeat would be his fault.

And what awaited him at home? How long would it be
before someone figured out that he hadn't killed the human
who'd crashed in his swamp? What did he have to offer in
counterbalance to that atrocity?

If, by the time anyone found out he'd spared an intruder,
he had already taught the humans how a single pilot could
deal with a four-seater Hyos gunship, well, who could
argue with any land holder doing what was necessary to
defend his land—even sparing an intruder?

Maybe something of his life could still be salvaged.

The circulating mass of humanity in the lobby area before
the Records counter had somehow jockeyed Indiw into a
line before a single clerk's station. He stared at the people
working behind the Records counter, only vaguely aware that

the hubbub dealt with the impending arrival of a resupply freighter with replacement personnel aboard. He definitely did not belong in this line.

He had no choice but to accept Lorton's suggestion and teach the humans. It would be the easiest way out. But he wanted to go home. Yet he shrank from what would happen if he did. Maybe if he stayed—just for a while. . . .

Chasing "maybes" was what had gotten him in such deep trouble last time. "Maybes," Falstaffs, and human females. That was the deadly mix. But so far there were no females involved in this. And it was a chance. Maybe his *only* chance to recoup his certain loss.

"Can I help you, sir?"

"Uh." He'd reached the head of the line. Indiw focused on the yeoman before him. "No, thank you. I've got everything I need."

Orders under one arm, he went to the Quartermaster.

They assigned him a cabin next to Falstaff. Naturally.

He didn't fight it. He had nothing against the boy, except that his very presence was terrifying.

Things went quickly after that. Apparently, orders had been passed concerning him. Nothing—absolutely nothing—could be done on a human ship without orders. Nobody was allowed to think for themselves. But somehow that wasn't as disturbing as it had been the first time he'd encountered it.

When he arrived at his cabin, humans were bustling in and out delivering equipment and supplies. Within two hours of his arrival, they'd brought in everything needed to make the tiny compartment into a comfortable habitat. Then he took possession with strategically placed scent markings.

There was a nice sand bed with an artificial sprinkler over it in place of a living tree. But the sap it delivered was real, and wondrously soothing to the hide. It made him realize how tired he was. He hadn't slept the previous night and he was close to collapse.

They'd brought him Ardr rations, and the means to store and heat them. He even got to choose the cuisine. The

uniforms all came with Pit Bull Squadron patches and
rank insignia in little bags ready to be pinned on. Toi-
letries, softly lined uniforms that wouldn't dull his hide,
scent-controlling devices, modified lighting fixtures, and
a complete library that contained everything on all four
of Sinaha's reading services made the cramped space into
a home.

They expected him to stay a lot longer than he did.

The debriefing was one of those formalized rituals used
by humans for pack bonding. It began with the humans
taking places around a long oval table and then rising to
assume identical postures as Lorton walked into the room
flanked by two women of lesser rank. Indiw rose but made
no effort to imitate the humans until he saw the women.

Then Indiw's claws twitched in response to the clear
and obvious threat. Though some of the other pilots were
female, they had paid him no attention. And there was a
Wing Commander female named Tagawa down the table
from him, but she was Alpha Wing. Lorton's two females
had more power over him since they obviously controlled
Lorton. Indiw strove to become inconspicuous, telling himself that his uniform, identical to the other pilots', would
help.

Falstaff arrived, late and panting, to slip into the chair
beside Indiw's. Lorton pretended not to notice. The women
did eye the latecomer penetratingly, though. Falstaff pretended not to notice. Indiw held his breath.

The proceedings began with bits of recordings lifted
from the fighters, and questions directed to the partners
of pilots who had died in the action. But very quickly
it centered on how Splinter Squadron had dealt with the
porky.

Porky, thought Indiw morosely. *Since a Pit Bull isn't a
bovine, I'll bet a porky isn't a swine, but then what is it?
Something blasphemous?*

"—as Commander Indiw will be telling you soon. Isn't
that right, Commander?"

"Sir?" Indiw had lost the thread of the discussion.

"In Simulator C at ten-hundred today," prompted Lorton.
The class!

Lorton waved his hand around the table—there were over twenty-five pilots at the table, and more on chairs around the edges of the room. "Your first students are ready."

Suddenly it was all horribly real. Humans.

Falstaff leaned close and muttered, "All you have to do is walk them through the logic steps that led you to develop that little program you zapped the porky with!"

Lorton smiled, nodded, and said happily, "That will be all." And he started out of the room.

"Tenshun! Dismiss!"

The coherence of the rigid grouping dissolved suddenly and re-formed as something else, just like a group of Ardr pilots breaking pattern to reweave into an offensive stance.

"Come on, Commander," urged Falstaff, "relax. It won't be hard. I'll help." He urged Indiw toward the door but politely refrained from physical contact. "I just wish you'd told me last night that you were staying. I'd have helped you work out a lesson plan—not that you don't know what you're doing, but I doubt you've ever taught humans before."

"No, I haven't."

"Don't worry about a thing. Everyone here's eager to learn your tricks. We've seen too many of our buddies killed by those porkies."

"What, exactly, does 'porky' mean? Why call a four-seat gunship such a thing?"

"Well, who could say 'four-seat gunship' while trying to shoot one down? So we call it what it looks like—a porcupine, bristling guns in every direction."

"Porkupine," said Indiw, resolving to look that one up.

"Yeah, but that's too long to say, too, so we just call it a porky. Simple, no?"

The human led the way into a lift filled with pilots from the debriefing. Indiw fell silent as he realized they were more nervous than he was. The lift stopped in an area of the ship Indiw had never explored on the old *Tacoma*. Class-rooms lined the hall, which ended in huge double doors labeled SIMULATOR C, AUTHORIZED PERSONNEL ONLY.

Falstaff led the mob of humans down that long corridor. Unobtrusively, he kept his body between Indiw and the others as he bragged over his shoulder about his new wingman's prowess at killing porkies.

The simulator room was gigantic. It consisted of eighty carrels facing a larger demonstrator's cockpit display set up on a stage so everyone could see it.

There were three men already in the room working at control panels in the walls near the door. As Indiw came in, one of them approached him, saluted, and presented a flight helmet labeled INSTRUCTOR. "Everything's ready for you, sir! We've got the memory from your fighter installed up front so you can run your demo anytime. If you need help with the controls, we'll be right here." He tapped the helmet phones.

Falstaff returned the salute and dismissed the man.

Five minutes later, half the room was filled. Indiw donned the helmet and climbed onto the stage with the huge model of cockpit instrumentation behind him. Looking down at the audience, he could barely make out the tops of his students' heads over their carrel walls.

The room was cooler than the rest of the ship's norm. His position put him in a nice breeze. His horns had become used to the dense effluvium of *human*. He was almost comfortable, but not enough to think how to go about this.

His helmet earphones came to life with Falstaff's voice. "Pit Bull Three to Pit Bull Four. Let's show 'em how we did it?"

As good a place to start as any. Indiw sat and swiveled to face the array of controls behind him. They were normal size models slaved to the huge replica the others could see. But there were two banks of controls he didn't recognize.

"Here," said one of the technicians, adjusting switches. "Now it'll run yesterday's battle. Use this to pause the action, and this to talk to all the carrels at once, or with this you can single out a pilot." He stepped back, and

Indiw's board flashed into the configuration showing as they encountered that porky.

With a little experimentation he began to see the arrangement made sense—if you insisted on trying to teach eighty pilots at once. *Humans. Pack hunters.*

He and Falstaff flew the final attack on the porky with Indiw pausing the action to explain each stage of his thinking as he analyzed the digital image of the monster and then as he applied his knowledge of his system's limits to the problem of that tiny vulnerability in the porky's defense.

Afterward, Indiw answered questions until he sounded hoarse and then the pilots left pounding each other on the shoulders, punching each other with closed fists, and laughing incongruously all the while.

From his seat on the stage, Indiw watched this form of pack-bonding ritual with icy fingers of terror gripping his vitals. Why did it make him feel so helpless?

One of the pilots lingered until Falstaff was alone, and then approached the young human. Indiw could hear clearly, though the humans probably didn't realize it.

"Ray, how in hell did you know what Commander Indiw wanted you to do on that last attack run? You hadn't discussed it. He admitted he'd never even heard of the porkies since they're so new on this part of the border. How did you know what to do?"

"Don, we're Pit Bull Squadron. It's that simple."

"But you'd never so much as flown together before."

"He flew with my uncle, and he was Pit Bull. I studied all the records. My uncle taught me everything he could as I was growing up. So I just *knew* what Commander Indiw had in mind, and I knew how to help."

The human, Don, nodded as if that explained it. Then he said a peculiar thing. "Do you think I could get a posting to Pit Bull?" No, not peculiar. Humans had to be assigned to squadrons. They needed orders. What was peculiar was Don's shy diffidence in asking.

"I don't know, Don. We are the best. Tina and Greg are a hard act to follow."

"So are you and Indiw, but I know I can do it. Put in a good word for me, will you?"

"Why don't you turn out and fly simulator with me tomorrow, say, oh-seven-hundred? Let's see what you can do."

Now that made sense to Indiw.

Somewhat relieved, Indiw left the two human pilots talking in the darkened simulator room. His orders said that his scheduled duties for the day were completed, except for reports on the class he'd just conducted and his plan for tomorrow's lesson, which should be filed with Captain Lorton before the hour of twenty. But before he could outline a lesson sequence, he had to have his program modules.

He went to the hangar deck where the engineers were supposed to be repairing his craft. He remembered that he, as a pilot, wasn't expected or allowed to work on his own machine, but he had to see what condition it was in. He had a flight to make.

When he got to the hangar, though, it was in an uproar. Stripped down skeletons and heaps of parts had been shoved to one side to make room for rows of cargotainers lined up in the work space. The engineers were cracking open the containers and carting off packages.

The resupply ship must have arrived. So where was his fighter? How could he find it? Get it launched? Once again, as so often among the humans, he felt helpless.

Then his eye fell on an oblate spheroid tucked into one corner of the deck. It took a few moments to recognize it out of context. A porky. More or less intact.

He looked it over, ran a hand across the scorched and burned areas. It was hardly damaged. This was a real treasure. Circling, he found an open hatch and climbed inside. Hyos stench filled the cramped compartment. He had to worm his way through to what had to be the pilot's seat.

He folded himself gingerly into the awkwardly shaped rack—Hyos had more joints in their limbs than humans and Ardr, and their arms were longer, their hands different.

Indiw had studied diagrams of the other Hyos craft. He played with the controls, discovering this craft was drained of power. He saw the control board links to the three other gunners stationed above him and to either side.

"Excuse me, Commander, but you're not allowed in here. Security, you know. Sensitive information."

Indiw turned. An armed woman wearing the braid that designated those who forced order on the unruly was leaning into the hatch, smiling. Indiw swallowed his terror. In his experience, the smiling human female was the most dangerous creature in the galaxy. All he needed was to be nominated for another award for heroism! He answered evenly, "Why would I not be allowed in here? There might be something of interest to learn."

"You have to have authorization. You're not on my list of those who have access."

On Sinaha, if someone had tried to block him from information, he'd simply have gutted the miscreant and had done with it. It took a few moments to stifle the impulse and think of an answer a human could accept. "Perhaps Captain Lorton would provide you with a solution to your problem if you asked him?" He tried to sound sympathetic.

"He doesn't have clearance. I'm sorry, Commander, but you'll have to leave. Regulations."

While he thought about that, Indiw asked, "How did this craft arrive here virtually undamaged?"

"Search and Rescue picked it up derelict after the battle. They say it just ran out of power."

Indiw swung back to inspect the power indicators. They were all dark. But there sure were a lot of them. No wonder the porky sported such robust shielding and such powerful weapons. He counted the power banks, trying to recall how much each one would store. He commented, "It would take all the housekeeping power that *Tacoma* uses in an hour to resupply this porky. How could they have run out of power?"

"How would you know that?" asked a deeper voice.

Indiw turned and found a white-clad technician leaning over the woman's shoulder. Indiw told him where he'd gotten his estimate. The woman complained that she hadn't been able to get the Pilot Commander to leave and would have to get her supervisor to issue the order and put Indiw on report.

The technician said, "Oh, don't bother. That's our new hardware expert. Go on back to work, Shirl. I'll get his clearances straightened out. He just didn't realize he needed to file the forms first. I'll stay with him. I want to hear more about this."

She shrugged and left. The man said, "I'm Captain Misholu. I run Flight Engineering Services for Delta Wing. Call me Sergei." He squeezed into the tiny compartment blocking Indiw's exit.

Every combative instinct triggered, Indiw replied with his own name, rank, and assignment.

"Don't worry about the clearances." Misholu waved a hand. Indiw aborted the urge to sever the member from the human's arm. "You're always welcome in my department, Commander. Your reputation has preceded you!"

"That's nice." And then his numb mind finally rendered up the proper formal phrase. "Captain, if you'll excuse me, I must go now. I've duties to perform."

Miraculously, it worked. Misholu backed out of the cramped space and left the exit clear for Indiw. "Well, I do hope you'll feel free to spend as much time on this craft as you like. I can get you released from other duties— uh, if that's what you'd prefer."

Relieved by the open space around them, Indiw realized the man was actually trying to be friendly, offering him a preference instead of an order. Some humans paid attention to the interspecies briefings. He got his heart rate under control and answered as graciously as he could, "My curiosity may overcome my good sense at the oddest hours. I would truly appreciate being allowed to study this craft—in my own way. I'm interested in what your experts discover."

"I'll see you get all the reports. I hope we'll be seeing a lot of you around here."

Indiw cast a glance over the porky. "*That* is certainly an inducement. Thank you, Captain—"

"Sergei."

"Sergei. Thank you." He retreated in good order, congratulating himself on sparing two more human lives. Their loss would have been more embarrassing than Falstaff's survival. The hangar deck was, after all, more theirs than his. And for all he knew, they were landed.

Then he remembered that they might not have known that he was landed, nor what that meant in terms of his right to kill. Humans. If his neighbors knew just how confused humans made him, they'd never accuse him of being tainted.

After an hour's search, he found his craft. It had been preflighted and set up in the launch bay. As he was checking it over, a squadron composed entirely of the new pilots who had arrived with the cargotainers came into the bay and took possession of four of the fighters. After some discussion among themselves and with launch control, they climbed into their machines and lined up for portage into the launch tube.

Indiw tagged along. Only after launch control queried him did he remember he was supposed to get orders before he could take a fighter out. In fact, he wasn't supposed to leave the ship without orders. Four years ago, Falstaff had made him spend an entire evening reading regulations—none of which had made sense. It was amazing he remembered as much as he did.

Vaguely, he wondered why Captain Lorton hadn't cleared the trip, and then he remembered how swamped Records had been what with the resupply arriving. Well with such a ponderous system, of course things didn't work right.

So when launch control assumed he was with the squadron just going out, he let them continue on that assumption.

In farewell, the man who cleared him for launch confirmed Indiw's assumption about Records, "Don't worry about the clearances, Commander. Records is swamped right now. Small wonder they're losing things. I'll have everything ready for you to sign when you get back."

"Thank you." Indiw hit his lock toggles and departed.

Once clear, he took orbit, contacted Sinaha ground control, and brought up a display of the local traffic between him and home. He chose a descent path, and in less than two hours was safely aground in his own backyard.

He had to get a considerable distance away from the craft before he could trust his nose, but a cursory inspection indicated that no one else had been here since he'd left. Good, maybe the dread news about his aberration wasn't common knowledge yet. People would be busy in the aftermath of the two battles and the renewed certainty that there were worse challenges yet to face.

He went in, packed the personal items he needed to take, then made a small bundle of things he couldn't justify taking into space but which he'd prefer to be able to repossess at some future time, whether he lost this land or not.

He took that bundle to the Walkway—public land he could access from a public gate, at peril to life and limb to be sure, but still possible. It was midday here, and the Walkway was deserted. He buried his belongings, carefully sprayed eradicator, and left.

Then he returned to the house, changed into a flight suit in a more reasonable color with a more comfortable cut, and extracted all his computer memory cores and programming reference texts. With his pack slung over his shoulder, he climbed back into his fighter.

Two hours later he'd installed his flight programs, triple-backing everything then testing, testing, testing. In the process, he outlined what to teach his eager humans over the next few weeks—if the Hyos granted them that much time. This evening all he'd have to do to finish his day's assigned tasks would be to write his report on today's class.

Feeling bright, eager, and very satisfied, he returned to orbit, locked on to *Tacoma,* and rode into the landing bay.

He was totally unprepared for the reception committee.

All the gracious, helpful, accommodating people who'd welcomed him had suddenly turned stone-cold and rigid with offense, and even anger.

Falstaff was there, standing in that awkward ceremonial posture, his eyes focused somewhere beyond Indiw as if

embarrassed to know him. Captain Lorton was there as
were his two women. A Records Officer stood behind
them beside a Launch Control engineer and two humans
with Delta Wing arm patches.

It was exactly what he'd have expected had he gutted
the armed woman and taken Captain Misholu's hand in the
porky.

Lorton's eyes traveled from Indiw's Ardr helmet—cut
to accommodate his horns where the human uniform was
not—down Indiw's Ardr flight suit to his broad toed boots.
Then he searched Indiw's face.

Indiw waited politely for an explanation.

At last Lorton asked, "Commander Indiw, had it occurred
to you that it was improper to take a fighter and leave the
ship without authorization?"

"Yes." Is *that* what this was all about?

"Commander, did you understand that you violated regulations?"

"Yes."

Lorton shook his head. "I don't believe this."

Falstaff said, "Captain, let me try. Please?"

"All right."

"Indiw, why did you take the fighter and leave the ship?"

"Because I had something important to do."

Lorton's eyes became wider and rounder.

"Mind telling us what that was?" asked Falstaff.

"I had to go home for a few minutes. After all, yesterday Captain Lorton told me *Tacoma* would be leaving the
vicinity soon. When was I supposed to go?"

The huge lump in Lorton's throat went up and down.

Falstaff said softly, "Commander Indiw, when you agreed
yesterday to come back to work on *Tacoma*, we assumed you
had agreed to abide by the rules and regulations that govern
the behavior of everyone else aboard this ship. We all feel
that our lives depend on the absolute commitment we all
share to those rules and regulations. When one of us violates
a rule, we all get very upset. We feel personally threatened."

Now *that* was what this was really about! "I see, Lieutenant Falstaff. Thank you for explaining the problem."

Lorton's crazed look vanished. "Good. Then I take it you won't do anything like this again in the future. It was all a simple intercultural misunderstanding?"

"But, Captain, I was only following your orders," protested Indiw, confused again. "If they were against regulations, I suggest you take it up with your superiors."

Lorton turned several shades paler. Falstaff said, "Captain Lorton, perhaps we could make more headway with this matter in a private discussion."

Indiw nodded in relief. "Good. You two discuss it. I have work to do." And he started around the group.

Falstaff cut him off by stepping in front of him and moving backward so as not to force a combat contact. Indiw stopped, waiting. Humans didn't usually settle their feelings of being threatened by killing one another, but if this was one of those occasions that warranted combat— well, it had been a long day. Even a mock combat would be nice after exposure to the pheromones on the Walkway.

"Commander Indiw, I meant that you, me, and Captain Lorton need to discuss this among the three of us."

From his tone, Indiw deduced that it must be a matter of some considerable urgency. "All right. I agree."

CHAPTER
THREE

★

WHEN THE DOOR TO A SMALL BRIEFING ROOM OFF THE
flight deck closed behind them, Lorton opened with a burst
of words. "All right, Commander, suppose you explain to
me where and when I ordered you to take a fighter down
to Sinaha's surface. Don't you know that's against the
treaty?"

"I'd never have taken an armed vehicle onto public
lands!" Indiw struggled not to show offense. This was a
misunderstanding. They'd get it straightened out. "I only
went home. How else was I supposed to get there?"

"I never ordered you to go home."

Falstaff murmured, "Captain, I doubt you specifically
ordered him not to."

"A good thing, too," said Indiw, temper winning out.
"Human blood makes a terrible mess."

Lorton choked.

Falstaff said, "Let's leave aside the question of your destination and talk about why you went there. What did you
go to do—if it's not too personal—that was so important?"

"To get the materials for the course I agreed to teach. I
have it all right here." Indiw slid his pack onto the table
and pulled out the case of computer memory. "While I was
reprogramming my fighter's memory, I blocked the lessons
for the course. I think it's really going to work!"

Falstaff's face underwent a transformation. "So *that's* it! You see, Captain, you did order Indiw to take a fighter and go home! You just didn't know it. You have to remember an Ardr thinks like a commander in chief. When he's accepted the responsibility for a task, he just does it whatever way he believes would be best. Indiw agreed to teach the course, so he assumed he was authorized to do whatever was needed."

"Indiw, is that true? Did you assume you had authorization for that little trip?"

"To be perfectly candid?"

"Please."

"I didn't make any assumptions. I didn't think about it at all. I realized there were authorizations missing only when I was already in the launch tube. And then I just assumed that by some—process I have never understood, someone would take care of it. Eventually. After all, I had to go and how else could I get there and back in time to teach tomorrow's course?"

"Oh, Commander," groaned Lorton. "I think I've done you an injustice."

"Really? I hadn't noticed."

Lorton shook his head as if he were dizzy. "Falstaff?"

"Sir!"

"Take your new wingman back to pilot's country and keep him out of trouble 'til he learns to go through channels."

"Sir! Let's go, Commander."

Indiw felt the human's touch whisper across the elbow of his flight suit. The human's other hand grabbed Indiw's pack. He must be frantic with some mysterious urgency to risk that touch. Indiw still held the case of computer cores but he could have beheaded the boy with a negligent swipe of his claws. He throttled the reflex, and a moment later he was in the corridor and approaching the lift at flank speed.

"My God, that was close!" gasped Falstaff in the lift. "Do you know that would have been the first time in recorded history a member of Pit Bull Squadron was court-martialed!"

Indiw felt as if the gravity had failed. His memory served up the list of horrible penalties the courts-martial were authorized to hand out. He had no idea which one applied to his crime, and no clear idea of what his crime was supposed to have been. "But the problem is cleared up now?"

"Yes. Captain Lorton won't press charges. He'll take care of everyone else. And if Sinaha doesn't come after us for an unauthorized landing, you're free."

"But I didn't make an unauthorized landing!"

"If you say so."

There was no way to get an authorization for anything on Sinaha. The very concept was so alien most people wouldn't know what you were talking about.

"This is our deck. Now, Lorton has made me responsible for you, so do I have your word that you'll go to your quarters and stay there until I come for you in the morning?"

"I hadn't planned to go anywhere else today."

"That isn't exactly what I asked. Do you agree to stay put until I come for you, or at least call me if you decide to go out? If you want to go work out or maybe go for a swim, I'll be right next door. We can go together to make sure you don't get into trouble."

Indiw was absolutely certain the young human was not making any sort of sexual advance. He'd learned recently that large groups of humans often shared immersion facilities without sexual activity, though in some cultures the sexes did not mix in the water.

As they reached their doors, Indiw turned to the human. "All right, I'll agree, if you'll promise me one thing."

"Which is?"

"Don't ever mention swimming to me again—and don't mention it to any other Ardr. Okay? Taboo topic."

"Ah. I didn't know. Amazing what xenologists can miss. Sorry. It's a deal." Uncertainly, he offered his open hand.

Indiw retracted his claws and took the hand briefly.

When his door closed behind him he felt a twinge of déjà vu. He dismissed it, heated rations, and set to work.

He couldn't spend his life comparing one Falstaff to the next. There would probably be an unending parade of them,

and unending troubles following in their wakes. He had to
concentrate on the trouble of the moment and let the future
and the past take care of themselves.

And the trouble of the moment kept escalating. On his
third day of classes, Indiw finished by having the whole
group fly a simulated mission. He, Falstaff, and two others
flew as Pit Bull. The enemy was a swarm composed of
twenty porkies and a hundred standard Hyos fighters.

They took fifty percent casualties, but they vanquished
the swarm. "Tomorrow," Indiw announced, "I'll show you
a new way to evade those cannon shots. They're so powerful, even a near miss can total you."

Falstaff had told him to snap out the word "Dismissed!"
to end the class, but however ceremonial the utterance it
still sounded like an order. When he turned and walked
toward the door, they generally all got the idea.

He saw Falstaff lower his head into his hands in despair,
but he kept on walking. He didn't make it though. One of
Lorton's women accosted him. This one was ranked Lieutenant Commander, a rank below Indiw's courtesy title.

She was of the darker-skinned variety of human with
softly rounded features that looked more like a work of
art than a face. But it didn't fool Indiw. A human female
in any guise was potential disaster.

He stopped far enough from her to give a polite bow of
greeting and stood with his hands carefully behind his back,
claws tightly sheathed. "Lt. Commander Vistula."

Her mouth tightened. "Pilot Commander Indeeyou," she
said, mispronouncing his name. He'd given up correcting
people. She handed him a data nodule color-coded as
Orders. "You're to fly in the memorial ceremony. It'll
be tight formation flying." She gestured to the room full
of empty simulators. "You had better practice."

She saluted crisply and left him breathless.

Falstaff came up behind him, saw the Orders nodule in
his open palm, and boomed joyfully, "Oh, you got tapped!
What an honor! They passed me over this time. Well, anyway Pit Bull will be represented and that's what's important."

Honor! Another female enemy. Dread washed through Indiw. All he needed to totally ruin his entire strategy for rescuing his life was another human female handing out human honors! But he had to ask. "What is a memorial ceremony? What kind of ceremony involves flying?"

"Oh, boy."

An hour later Indiw knew more than he ever wanted to know about human military tradition and ceremony. He didn't understand it, but as he read through the material Falstaff drew from the databanks for him, trying to memorize the parts that pertained to honoring the dead, he had random flashes of insight. There was some oblique connection between military ceremony, the way humans made pictures in the sky, and whatever it was that motivated humans to contend and compete.

But it all went by him in a confusing whirl. For the next six days Indiw taught for two hours each morning, flew simulator with Falstaff and the candidates for Pit Bull, spent time with the derelict porky and got it repowered, then worked evenings under Falstaff's guidance on procedures and ceremonies. He also flew the simulator's special tight formation drill that his part in the ceremony would require.

Until the last moment, he hadn't tried to get out of it. After all, who would ever know? Now, he regretted that.

Head crammed with the stringent rules governing the day's events, Indiw drew his freshly painted fighter into the launch tube behind three other pilots. Though they were flying with Pit Bull's insignia, he had no idea who they were. No one ever explained how these decisions were made or asked his opinion or his agreement.

Falstaff would watch from the hangar deck with all the other people on *Tacoma*. He was involved in preparing for another ceremony to follow this one. Indiw didn't envy him. While Indiw flew, the human would stand or sit in that absurd tense posture for hours while various people talked.

The speeches would be made available to everyone on Sinaha, not that anyone would listen. He hoped. *Tacoma* had left to patrol a day's radius from Sinaha but had returned for this ceremony to honor the dead of both human and Ardr. Normally, Ardr just ignored the bizarre human antics such occasions precipitated. They seemed harmless, if wasteful.

The humans always invited Ardr pilots to fly in these tributes, but nobody ever did. Indiw had ignored those invitations himself for so long, he'd forgotten about them until he'd studied the memorial from the human point of view. But this time some Ardr might notice because in the speeches humans would point out that for the first time an Ardr pilot would fly the missing-man formation.

Not only that, but they had arranged to fly the formation not only over *Tacoma,* but down into atmosphere, over one of the large population centers. Thank goodness it was on an island far from any held land. Nobody important would be likely to notice. He hoped.

He had learned of the speeches mentioning him and of the dip into atmosphere just before he hoisted himself into his craft. He'd had no chance to protest, not that it would have done any good. He sensed a female's hand behind it all. The last time he'd tried to thwart a human female's intentions, he'd almost lost everything that made life worth living. He had no choice but to go through with this.

In rapid order, his squadron launched. They flew to the rendezvous, the three humans flying as Pit Bull exchanging personal comments, leaving him alone except for routine.

There had been so much damage to *Tacoma* fighters that only fifty were both fit to perform these close-order drills and good-looking enough for the ceremony. Still they made an impressive display as they grouped into a formation of formations, keeping station until *Tacoma* signaled.

Then they made their atmosphere dip, arrowing across the open sea. Buffeted by each other's wakes, they held their tight formation until they crossed the perimeter of the island, then, over the town, one fighter from each squadron rose up and arced away from the formation. The formation flew on, steady and straight, skimming near the tops of the trees that sheltered the population of unlanded Ardr.

Indiw was the one who left his squadron. He watched from far above as the formation, complete with ridiculous-looking holes, moved in stately procession in full view of nobody in particular. Most of the Ardr dead who were presumably being honored had likewise been unlanded, neither their lives nor their deaths of consequence.

Even when a landed Ardr died the only consequence of note was that some youth might become landed. It was beyond Indiw why anyone but those whose status changed would care.

Still, it was quite a spectacular piece of flying. From his vantage high above it, Indiw imprinted the image on his memory. It was one thing to read about it, practice it in simulation, but something else to watch the solemn execution.

He met the formation in orbit, and they repeated the stunt on cue from *Tacoma,* this time in the tighter formation permitted in vacuum. On cue, Indiw peeled off and circled above the carrier, close to the open door of the hangar deck, which was shielded now only by a force screen.

Just for a moment, as the rest of the formation moved in stately procession past the opening, Indiw glimpsed the ranks of identically clad humans all raising their hands in salute, all in perfect unison. That was another image engraved on his memory with a shiver of real terror.

Humans were descended from pack hunters. Ardr were descended from lone hunters. On their native world, humans had exterminated all the lone-hunter species and domesticated most of the pack hunters.

Four years ago, Walter Falstaff had convinced Indiw that the human threat was not imminent because humans were evolving toward individualism, so humans would not have to kill or dominate Ardr. But all he'd learned since, including this military ceremony, indicated otherwise. Or seemed to. He had thought his understanding of humans had improved, but his every experience this time indicated his grasp of their motives was dangerously incomplete.

Indiw had been excused from attending the dining-in at which the memorial services would be concluded. Someone who issued orders must have remembered that Ardr do not eat in public. But Falstaff was responsible for setting up the large dining room for the occasion, and at the last minute one of his helpers fell ill. Indiw found himself placing awkward cutlery along the edge of a table facing a room full of tables while other humans ran around shouting.

He tried not to flinch and crouch at each loud voice.

"Indiw!"

He jumped and a handful of cutlery clattered to the table knocking over a crystal glass, which shattered.

"Shit!" said Falstaff, coming up to survey the damage. "I'll clean that up. Here, you take this rose and put it on that table in the back, the little one with the black cloth."

Indiw took the bud vase, inured to the human custom of destroying shrubbery to use as decoration, and searched for the designated table. The table set along one side of the hall with a large bowl and matching cups was draped in white like all the other tables. His eye scanned to the back of the hall. "Where? There?"

"Yes," said Falstaff, brushing broken glass into a heap.

It was a very small table, with one chair.

"I don't understand. I thought all the important people were supposed to sit up here."

"Indiw, the most important people of all sit at that table back there. Tonight, they are our honored guests."

"But there's only one place set."

"You just don't get it, do you? That's the missing man in the missing-man formation. That's the symbolic place set for all those who can't be here tonight—because they've served their time, or because they gave their lives that others might survive. Even though they're not here, they're with us always. Everyone who's ever been with us is with us tonight. This afternoon, I answered muster for my buddies who died in that last battle. They're gone, but they're still with us. If I have to, someday I'll answer for you. And I hope you'd answer for me, if it comes to that.

"There's been a Pit Bull Squadron flying since before humans first made it into space—and there always will be one. There are hundreds of us, Indiw, thousands, serving in an unbroken tradition of excellence, Pit Bull Squadron."

Indiw suppressed a shudder.

"There's no way you can grasp that, is there? And yet you're a part of it. You have the tradition from my uncle, whether you know it or not. All I've asked is that you pass it on to me." Falstaff took the bud vase. "Never mind. I'll do this. You can go now. And thanks for your help."

Indiw never remembered the long walk back to his place. His mind was filled with hordes of humans stretching back to the dawn of time, all saluting in unison, eyes glittering like Falstaff's had—both Falstaffs. Humans weren't pack hunters. They were something totally different. They hunted with their dead.

What a concept. It was eerie. Walter Falstaff would be in that room tonight feasting with his squadron, with his nephew. Indiw shut his door behind him and shut his mind to the whole subject. He didn't *want* to understand. He just wanted to rest. No, he wanted to go home.

He thought about it. He'd done what he'd stayed to do—started the pilots exploring the new limits of the fighter's systems. Some of them were already coming up with ideas he'd never thought of. They didn't need him anymore.

On an Ardr ship, having completed the responsibilities he'd taken on, he could have entered his resignation in the computer, and then just left. He could have landed a disarmed Ardr fighter on public land, set the beacon, and someone would have come to pick it up.

Here, he'd have to settle matters with the Records Officer who would create tedious regulations to delay him. If he just took a fighter again, there'd be reprisals. He was trapped until the Records Office opened again tomorrow.

With every fiber of his being yearning to sever all ties with humans, Indiw curled up on his sand bed to wait.

Inevitably, he fell asleep.

He woke to a nerve-shattering racket. It took several moments before he remembered he wasn't home. The ship lurched and began vibrating rhythmically. Weapons deploying. Fighters launching. The screeching din was the alert scrambling all pilots. They were under attack.

Falstaff's words formed on his lips. "Oh, shit."

In his mind, Indiw had resigned last night.

But *Tacoma* didn't know that. His fighter would be slotted for launch as if he were on his way at a full run. And, remembering how few craft were in tip-top condition, Indiw knew they couldn't afford not to have every one of them out there. They'd almost lost the last two battles. If this was another full-strength Hyos swarm . . .

He was halfway into his flight suit before he realized he'd decided to fly. He got what briefing he could from the screen in his quarters, and was out the door still stomping one foot into his boot, sealing up as he ran.

Falstaff came tearing along the corridor behind him, pulling his flight suit closed over a fragment of his formal wear. "It's a big one, Indiw," he called as he drew abreast. "It's as if they knew we'd be standing down. We're going to need everything you've taught us to save Sinaha this time."

"That's why I taught you."

"Oh," answered the youth, sidling through the big doors onto the hangar deck. "Here I thought you just liked standing up on the stage!"

He's teasing. He must be nervous.

Many other pilots dashing for their craft had also discarded various bits of formal wear as they sealed up their flight suits. So the ceremony hadn't concluded yet.

But there had been pilots on duty. Already several squadrons had launched, and the whump-chump of launches continued rhythmically. Indiw found his fighter, altogether too close to the front of the line. He had no time to make his usual last-minute checks. But he had checked everything out when he landed after flying the formations.

His gauges showed he'd been refueled. He jammed his helmet on, sealed his cockpit, and reported in as he brought his systems on-line.

A vaguely familiar female voice identified itself as Pit Bull One. She dictated the countdown and, after launch, pulled them together. *Tacoma* assigned them a target and they were off, streaking through space beside six other squadrons.

Indiw had no time to assess the entire battle, but he saw immediately what his end of it was all about. An entire phalanx of porkies was escorting a large cargo carrier, and boring directly for Sinaha, ignoring *Tacoma*.

That wasn't typical of a swarm escorting a Breeder to ground. It took only a few moments to calculate what the Hyos were after. They resisted being shoved into orbits that would put them to ground near arable land, or within striking distance of a population center. They were targeted on Tantigre Peak, and the experimental cannon emplacement.

Indiw was with those deployed to prevent that landing.

"Pit Bull One, this is Pit Bull Four. Have you been briefed on the Hyos's objective?"

"No, except that Intelligence got no warning they were coming. Our job is to keep them off the planet's surface. You got a problem with that?"

"No. But there's something I think you—"

Abruptly, Indiw was in the dogfight of his life.

They'd faced down three porkies by the time he realized these pilots were his top students. But it didn't take the Hyos long to figure out that the porkies had lost their edge. They regrouped and began slicing the attacking human force into bite-size chunks.

The humans responded by eating holes in the Hyos defensive lines and rejoining into a single formation. Before long, Pit Bull had a porky surrounded and cut off, but they were skimming Sinaha's atmosphere. "This is Pit Bull One. Pit Bull Four, it's your turn. We'll cover you."

Indiw faded back behind Falstaff and they began their run, just as they'd done it the first time.

But by now, this porky's crew had seen this maneuver succeed against their compatriots. Still, they tried what had always failed. They focused fire on the two attackers who were standing off to the other side and pounding them, ignoring the approaching pair.

Pit Bull One took a direct hit from their porky and then a Hyos fighter's missile slammed into her. The orange fireball lit up the sparse atmosphere, and when it cleared Pit Bull One was gone.

Pit Bull Two went for the Hyos fighter. Their target porky slammed three high-powered cannon blasts into Two's shields. The Hyos fighter scattered blob-shot in his wake.

Indiw had no idea why the humans called it blob-shot. It was a small deformable magnetic bottle almost like a soap bubble, though not round. Blob-shot deformed into many colors and shapes, but if it hit a defensive shield, it erupted into wild, searing energy. Most of it was too small to be more than a nuisance, but in battle even a small nuisance could destroy a fighter.

Firing missiles, Pit Bull Two flew into the curtain of blob-shot. His shields danced with blob splatter. Falstaff and Indiw held their approach vector steady on the target porky waiting for the cannon to fire. But from the porky's other side, its slicer flared and Two's shields erupted in sizzling green sparks.

Careening wildly, Two veered toward the planet in an uncontrolled power dive. Belatedly, Two's missiles connected, and the Hyos fighter spun out of control.

The target porky finally cleared its nearby cannon port. Falstaff went in hammering the porky's shields, then peeled off, leaving Indiw a clean target. Indiw fired.

The target porky made an audible explosion. They were much too low in atmosphere. Indiw climbed. Pit Bull Two's transponder wasn't registering at all.

Falstaff circled back and clung just off Indiw's wing as they climbed out of atmosphere, straining every seam against gravity and atmospheric turbulence.

"Oh, God!" groaned Falstaff.

Indiw spotted the Hyos cargo vessel and its escort, heavily beset by humans. As he watched, four porkies detached from that elite escort and converged on Pit Bull, leaving a hole in the cargo vessel's defense. They'd been targeted as that serious a threat.

Even as he watched, two other porkies detached from the escort and joined the pursuit of the remnants of Pit Bull.

"Come on, let's get out of here!" suggested Indiw. "Draw them away so the others can get that cargo hauler."

"Doesn't look like a Breeder ship!"

"Isn't." The other pilots didn't know the cargo vessel was the only important target in this battle because of "security"—i.e. nobody knew everything necessary to make intelligent choices so that everyone would feel insecure.

Pack hunters! he swore, even as he noted how Falstaff swooped in close behind him and stuck as Indiw climbed high above the atmosphere, above the battle, above the sleeting rain of particles from the battle.

"Indiw, behind us!"

"I see them," he said, driving away from the fight. One of the pursuers gave up, leaving only five. Or maybe he hadn't given up. Maybe he was going for reinforcements, not liking the odds. Or maybe he was low on fuel.

"What are you doing?" asked Falstaff.

"Thinking. What are you doing?"

"Shaking."

"Not yet, young one. You wanted to learn about Pit Bull traditions? Well, then, stick with me."

He broke into the dodging, swooping flight pattern of a novice weave, just to see what Falstaff would do.

To Indiw's surprise, the boy stuck with him, weaving the second craft's part of the pattern without a mistake.

"I didn't know you could do that," said Indiw.

"I got pretty good with the simulator, but I never had anyone to do it with for real."

"What level can you fly?"

They were arrowing away from the battle at top speed. They weren't outpacing their pursuers. But they weren't losing the race either.

"I can fly second level both offense and defense. I lose it at third level."

"Hmm. If you crash into me, there goes Pit Bull Squadron. But I think it's worth a try."

"What's worth a try?"

"Normally it takes a fourth- or fifth-level offensive weave to confuse Hyos, but they'll never expect human craft to weave pattern around them."

There was a silence. Indiw could almost see the young Falstaff tuck one lip between his white teeth. Then the boy said, "You're on. Lead the way, Pit Bull Four."

"All right. This one is called Inturirr. It's the lowest-level offensive weave. The object is to get your opponents to crash into each other—but not while you're between them." It was a child's game called Five-to-Two, but Indiw didn't mention that.

"Sounds simple enough. I'm ready when you are."

Indiw executed a long loop, then led the way back toward the pursuers, laying a straight course directly for the one in the lead. "When I say break, weave left, then do thinsor turns to your right, five, ten, then fifteen degrees, but increase your speed ten percent every fourth turn. Keep it up until I say break again. Then go straight up, maximum speed. Can you do that?"

"No problem."

If the Hyos hadn't been listening, and if they hadn't understood what he'd just said, it might work. But then Hyos had never yet been known to crack the electronic coding systems the Tier forces used. *It's got to work.*

They closed on their pursuers. Indiw held the straight course to the very last second, then told Falstaff, "Break!" and peeled off to the right as the human went left.

The porkies fired, but neither Pit Bull craft was hit.

Indiw wove the complement to Falstaff's pattern.

Two porkies fired on him simultaneously and hit each other. He was not between them. Neither was Falstaff.

In the moment of Hyos confusion, Indiw placed a lucky shot and nailed one of the Hyos. The fireball engulfed a nearby porky. He'd lost sight of Falstaff in the particle soup. Ticking off Falstaff's position with the trained clock inside his head, Indiw unloaded three missiles into the engulfed ship, hoping to keep its screens whited out a few seconds longer. Tick. Tick. *Come on, Falstaff!*

And the whited-out porky crashed splendidly into its neighbor, which had been forced to dodge Falstaff, thus putting itself right on target.

The shock wave of the dual explosion sent Falstaff tumbling out of his weave spot. He hadn't anticipated what was about to happen. Indiw compensated by breaking pattern and weaving a fourth-level offensive maneuver around the two remaining porkies until Falstaff yelled, "What the hell are you doing!" and fell in on his tail.

"Trying to stay alive," answered Indiw as he dropped out of the pattern to weave at the human's level again. "Can you weave inverted firsul?"

"I don't remember what that is!"

The two surviving Hyos had recovered. They spewed dense fire all around themselves, apparently hoping to hit the elusive enemy by sheer chance. There was no time to explain. "Do the opposite of what I do! Break."

Indiw sent his fighter into a full power run directly at the two remaining porkies. They separated, dodging.

Falstaff shouted, "Chicken porkies! I love it."

Indiw yelled, "Break," and sheared off to the left, hoping Falstaff would go right. He did.

"Now, break again, toward me."

They approached each other, passed, looped, and circled one of the porkies. It got off one lucky shot and grazed Indiw's shields, knocking him out of the pattern.

Indiw danced back into place, holding his breath, hoping Falstaff would have moved. He had. They didn't collide.

Falstaff was good. Confidently, Indiw began the next firsul weave, inverting the pattern around the center between the two Hyos craft. "On break, go straight up at max."

"Acknowledged."

The pattern brought them to the outside, with both Hyos between them. Indiw pounded his Hyos, driving it back and back toward its partner. Just as the Hyos cannon port opened for fire, Indiw acquired it and fired. Missed.

The Hyos finally got a lock on him with its slicer, and his shields screamed under the strain.

But he held on. The clock in Indiw's head that kept track of Falstaff's position ticked steadily, but his instruments had lost the human again.

The two porkies edged toward each other. Indiw had another clean shot at a cannon portal open for firing. He missed. The Hyos cannon shot grazed his shields, already sizzling from the slicer's nibbles.

At last, Indiw's pattern took him below his porky. He hoped Falstaff wouldn't be in the way. He wasn't. Indiw goosed his porky's underside, slipped between the two porkies, then up and around the outside of Falstaff's porky.

As it was designed to do, that thread of the weave broke the slicer out of its lock. The slicer almost cut through the other porky's field before the Hyos doused his beam.

"Falstaff, watch out for that one's slicer," warned Indiw, unsure the human could hear him through the tightly overlapping battle shields and weapons noise. With one hand, he brought up one of his prize programs. He had to get back to the real battle. If the Hyos got that cannon . . .

But his plan was working. Just a couple more seconds. If he had the nerve, and if Falstaff had grasped the pattern, there was even a slim chance they might both survive this.

When the mental clock ticked over, and he knew Falstaff ought to be clear, he wove back over the top, slid between the two porkies, delivered a resounding farewell slap with his cannon, and wove around his own porky again, keeping it busy with a barrage of small missiles.

The two porkies edged closer together. Their defensive shields were almost overlapping. They didn't want either human craft between them. That was how they'd lost their compatriots.

Finally, the weave took him close enough to Falstaff to acquire the audio link. "All right, Falstaff, break."

Falstaff went straight up. Indiw slid between the two porkies, engaged his little program, and waited. His craft stopped as if looking for Falstaff, accidentally presenting a perfect target. Both porkies cleared cannon ports for fire. Indiw's program fired on both of them, slammed his shields to max, and simultaneously threw him down and clear.

Not quite clear.

The stupendous explosive power in two porkies smashed into his shields like a fist. He lost attitude control.

"Indiw!"

He fought, almost had it, lost it. Something was wrong. He killed all his power, went ballistic. Then he brought up his attitude computer. Scrambled.

Dizzy with Coriolis forces spinning his balance centers, Indiw fumbled into the compartment behind his seat, found the catches on the access port, and in the dark, by touch alone, clumsy in his gloves, he pulled the board from the attitude computer and substituted his fire-control board.

Sparks erupted through the cockpit. He completely wrecked his environmental instrument display, but the attitude display straightened out.

Little by little, he nursed the fighter back to stability and brought his communications on-line again.

He was alone in space.

He had never expected that.

Falstaff, the original Falstaff, would never have abandoned him.

Maybe Falstaff had been killed while Indiw was out of touch? He searched. But there was no derelict around, no *Tacoma* transponder signal nearby.

He extended his sensors back toward *Tacoma* and found the rest of the battle had ended, too. At least the carrier was still alive and calling its fighters home. He wondered if that meant they'd won. What had happened to that cargo ship?

He set course for *Tacoma*, not sure if he wanted to find Falstaff back there alive or not. He'd thought he understood the boy.

But then, if he'd learned to weave pattern like an Ardr, maybe he'd begun to think like an Ardr. Maybe he just chose to leave. Now there was a chilling thought.

Nursing his crippled fighter along, Indiw didn't even try to report in to *Tacoma*. His communications panel was half dark. Substituting that board hadn't been such a wonderful idea. Maybe some redesigning was in order.

Out of the hazy, sparkling distance came four bright white shapes. Their transponder symbols were red plus signs.

★
CHAPTER
FOUR
★

IN THE FOREFRONT OF THE WHITE CRAFT CAME A BAT-
tered, seared fighter—a familiar fighter.

"Indiw, is that you? Pit Bull Four?" The voice crackled
in Indiw's ears.

"This is Pit Bull Four."

"Are you all right? Can you make it back by yourself?"

"I can make it back."

"Good!" Indiw's audio-scanner locked on and followed
Falstaff's voice onto another band. "Okay, fellas, this is
my buddy. You can go rescue someone who needs it.
Thanks."

Indiw heard the farewells as the white craft peeled off
and returned to the battlefield.

Falstaff joined him, nestling up to his right flank. "Boy,
you had me scared. What happened?"

*He went for help. Perfectly reasonable action from a
human point of view, or an Ardr's.* Indiw explained what
he'd done to regain control.

"You know what? You're nuts! And you know what
else? You're going to catch it from Captain Lorton for that
damnfool stunt."

Indiw was silent.

"Commander, you hear me? Sir?"

"I heard you."

"What's the matter, Indiw?"

"I don't understand humans and I'm no longer sure I even want to try." Ray Falstaff sounded angry, which made no sense to Indiw. It just made him feel detached, as if he were ill.

"You're just tired. That was a helluva battle, and we were short on sleep even before spending the night fighting our tails off. But I tell you, flying with you has been an *education*. Now I'd never want anyone else on my wing, and I don't care how much that displeases Captain Lorton."

On balance, Indiw felt the same way. Flying with Falstaff had felt very, very good. He was better than the original. Much better.

But Lorton did seem very displeased.

The Wing Captain marched into the debriefing with his face carved in stone. However, his anger did not seem to be directed at Pit Bull. In fact, he briskly set aside the usual ceremonial dissection of the battle and said, "Delta Wing has been given a new assignment. For the duration, you are all subject to top security. You will not speak a word of this matter to anyone—not even your pillow-partners, even if they are Delta Wing, too. You'll find the requisite forms to sign on your display screens."

Everyone reached to mark the screens. As each signature registered, the screen would start flashing. Falstaff urged Indiw to sign his screen. "It won't stop until everyone's signed. The Captain can't continue until we're wrapped."

Indiw wrote his name. The screen did not start flashing. Falstaff said, "Use Ardr script the way you do signing requisitions—it's your official signature." Indiw complied and the screen flashed three times in unison with all the others, and then the screens all went black. His came on with a red sign saying SECURED.

"Thank you. Now that the room is secured," said Lorton, "I can tell you that Delta Wing—what's left of it—is no longer a combat wing. We are now dedicated to Reconnaissance. Your craft are already being altered to carry recorders, extra fuel, and power for sensor arrays and stealth circuits. You will also have needle-beam burst transmitters."

Indiw ignored Lorton. He still didn't know what had happened to the Hyos cargo ship. As soon as he finished the resignation formalities, he'd be home, able to learn anything he wanted. Then he could figure out how to answer for his aberrant behavior toward the human trespasser.

"Pilot Commander Indiw!"

Indiw's attention snapped back to Lorton. "Sir?"

"True we don't know much about the stolen weapon, but it might be wise of you to listen to what we do know."

"Stolen?" Indiw sat up, claws snapping out and in.

"By the Hyos. During the battle. Even the fact that it's missing is top secret, as well as its nature. It is customary to listen at briefings."

Falstaff moved as if to defend Indiw, but Indiw forestalled him. "Did you say the cannon was stolen? That the Hyos cargo ship got through to Tantigre Peak?"

"You knew what that cargo ship came for?"

"I guessed. After all, what else is there on Tantigre Peak?" To himself, he added, "And after it proved so effective, too." He'd failed to protect the cannon. He was acutely aware of the humans turning to look at him, alarm growing as they realized he had failed monstrously. "The Hyos have nothing like that cannon. It operates on a completely new principle based on—"

"That's a top-secret weapon!" snapped Lorton. "Your people wouldn't even tell us what it does—what is it, Falstaff?"

"Uh, sir, if I understand correctly, the Ardr don't have anything vaguely resembling the concepts *top security* or *top secret*. Or any kind of secret for that matter."

Lorton paused to digest that, probably remembering the endless cross-species briefings he'd drowsed through. "Then why wouldn't they tell us about it?"

"Indiw?" prompted Falstaff.

Because you're the enemy, thought Indiw, *potential enemy anyway.* Aloud, he made a better guess, "Probably because the person you asked didn't know, didn't care, and figured they had better things to do than do research for lazy people."

"Commander Indiw, is there anything you can tell us about the weapon—without offending your own people?"

"Of course. I know all about it, but I don't exactly understand it. They only began building it two years—"

"Two years, and our intelligence service has never heard of it?" Lorton blurted, then looked embarrassed and a bit glassy-eyed with shock and bewilderment.

"Well, nobody knew if it would work until the attack that destroyed *Katular,* and then the cannon lost power after its first volley. But it did work that first time!"

"How would you know?"

"I saw it."

"You mean the weapon is public knowledge on Sinaha?"

"I doubt it. Very few would understand it. I surely don't. But I was interested because it's based on my work."

"Your work?"

He waved a hand and said, "Just the work I've done on fighter's circuitry design." Indiw was not about to remind them of the "act of heroism" for which he'd been given the Croninwet Award, when he'd used his fighter's cannon to transfer momentum to Falstaff's crippled fighter and incidentally burned out his own fighter's systems in a very peculiar way. His peers had declared his actions to be a mistake and the maneuver to be suicidal, warning all pilots away from it. The humans had singled him out for an award and nearly destroyed everything he'd worked for all his life.

"Oh." Lorton favored Indiw with a penetrating stare. The room was so rife with the odor of stressed human that Indiw could not discern Lorton's personal odor, but the Captain's voice was tight as he said, "Lt. Falstaff, please be sure Commander Indiw has a complete briefing on *Security*—with particular emphasis on the elementary concepts an Ardr might overlook, such as the concept *traitor*."

"Yes, sir!"

"As for the rest of you, you are to forget that you have heard what Commander Indiw has just said."

While Indiw was busy with the idea that a human could obey an order to forget what they'd just learned—something that might even save their life never mind their land—

Lorton outlined Delta Wing's new mission.

Indiw missed the details, grasping only the general outline of Lorton's remarks. Delta Wing was responsible for finding the cannon, and Alpha Wing under Captain Tagawa would then either recapture it or destroy it. Delta Wing was now under the command of the Rear Admiral who directed all Intelligence Operations on this border. The pilots were ordered to rest and be ready to fly within sixteen hours.

As the meeting broke up, Indiw made for the corridor, turning toward the lifts that would take him to the Records Officer. Then he paused. Should he resign now? He had been one of those who had failed to protect the cannon. There was no telling what the Hyos could do with it.

"No, this way, Indiw." Falstaff stopped at his elbow.

"No," he said. He couldn't show his face on Sinaha yet, but if he was to have a strong enough argument to get him out of this mess, he had to fly with Alpha Wing. He had to get the cannon back. "I have to see the Records Officer."

"Indiw!" Falstaff danced along beside him as he bore toward the lifts. "You can't resign now. I—"

"I'm a fighter pilot, not a recorder jockey. I choose to join Alpha Wing."

"Commander Indiw, please stop and listen for a moment."

There was desperation in the human tone. Indiw stopped.

"I suspect there's something you don't understand here." He dropped to a near whisper. "You have a remarkable amount of information *about* humans, but you don't seem very practiced at thinking with that information."

"What have I missed?" asked Indiw, likewise quietly.

"Well, I'm not very good at applying what I know of Ardr, so I don't know exactly how to put this. But, Indiw, you can't *trust* humans the same way you trust Ardr."

"What a remarkable thing to hear a human say."

The fair skin gained a pinkish hue. "I don't think you've thought about what your request to move to Alpha would *look* like—to a traitor. I bet you could recite the dictionary definition of traitor, but I also bet you couldn't spot one even if he offered you a bribe."

Falstaff was right. Indiw knew of only one case where a human had accepted items of value from the Hyos in return for disarming First Tier defenses. It had lost them a world. He had always assumed the human had been mentally ill.

He leaned against the bulkhead. "Go ahead. Explain."

Falstaff eased closer and dropped his voice to a softer whisper. "*If* there were a traitor on this ship—or even if not and there is one somewhere in the upper echelons of Records Division—just *one* traitor who noticed that right after the debriefing, you ran to Records to ask for reassignment, they would *know* that Alpha Wing had been tapped to recapture the stolen weapon. Indiw, if you do this, *you* will be a traitor. You'd be guilty of breaking security."

The sensation that washed through Indiw was akin to that which he'd felt after he'd almost seen images in the sky.

"Yeah, I thought you hadn't considered that. Lorton put us under full security wraps. Every one of us has to watch our every word, every gesture, every move. And we watch each other for slips. It has to be business-as-usual for the next sixteen hours. That means eat, sleep, get ready to fly. And that's all—except *you*'ve got to study security procedures, starting with the reason for them!"

"How do you know there wasn't a traitor in the room?"

"Indiw!" The human recoiled, then returned, whispering. "Look, we're all buddies. We've lived together and risked our lives together. We *know* each other. We *trust* each other—maybe better than Ardr trust each other. You and the two replacements who survived that battle are the only strangers among us, the ones the rest of us would suspect if anything leaked. Indiw, just someone filing a suspicion against you could ruin everything you've worked for."

"But—I'm Ardr—"

"Listen to me. There's maybe one human in a hundred who's paid attention to the behavior profiles of Ardr during cross-species briefings. And most of them don't believe it. It simply isn't *plausible* that among twenty billion Ardr there isn't one who'd sell out."

"Not plausible?"

"No."

Well, in that case humans would never, ever, suspect that Ardr regarded humans as a menace that would, one day, have to be eradicated in a fight of extermination. Of course, nothing would start until the Hyos were out of the picture, and that was unlikely within the next few centuries.

"Indiw?"

"Do I understand this correctly? If I choose to fly with Alpha Wing, I'll be signaling a hypothetical traitor who might deduce that Alpha Wing was designated to recover the weapon. That might give the Hyos a chance to strike at Alpha Wing before they reach target. If I chose to take such a risk, I'd be suspected of signaling the Hyos on purpose."

"Not to mention you'd be guilty of disregarding orders and breaking security—minor charges compared to espionage. Indiw, your knowledge of the weapon would be indictment enough—most espionage agents are insiders. Or if your expertise becomes known, then you could be a kidnap target."

"Kidnap?" Another bizarre compound word. His mind was blurred with fatigue. He just couldn't cope with this.

"The Hyos could capture you and force you to tell or hold you for ransom."

Indiw struggled to digest that.

"Courting that danger would be a traitorous act."

He couldn't follow it. "I must be very tired."

"A while back you said you were tired of trying to figure humans out, and neither of us have had any sleep in a couple of days. Culture shock is treacherous, and Ardr are as susceptible as humans. I'm trying to make it a little easier on you, that's all."

"Easier?" Indiw used the human's other name as he'd heard others use it. "Ray, do me a favor. Stop trying."

"All right. Let's—"

A passing human slapped Falstaff's shoulder, knocking him off balance. "Hey, Ray! Gettin' a little cozy there, no?"

Indiw backed off reflexively, claws out, ready to defend his partner.

Not noticing Indiw's reaction, Falstaff laughed and hit the other human on the back, then grabbed him and they engaged in a shoving match that Indiw finally recognized as a mock battle. Exchanging nonsensical comments, they ended slapping each other on the open palms. Then the human walked off. The whole encounter hadn't lasted thirty seconds.

Falstaff turned to find Indiw straightening, panting. "Relax, Commander. Jack was just teasing. You won't find many pilots who respect Ardr flying the way he does."

"I understood he did not intend you serious harm."

"But if he had, you'd have gutted him?"

"No. I'm still wearing flight boots." It would have been nice, though. It was a bit frightening how very nice the thought seemed. Indiw turned his back on Falstaff and strode off toward his own place, his claws digging deeply into the padding in his boots. His hand claws wanted to sink into a human throat and yank until the head came off.

Washing, changing, eating, drinking, Indiw thought hard about the battle, how wonderful it had been to fly with a Falstaff again, and about the young Falstaff's intriguing ability with pattern weaving.

What would other Ardr make of a human who could weave pattern? He was sure they'd hear of it. After all, it had happened during the key part of the battle where the cannon prototype had been lost.

Choosing to fly with this human in the first place would be difficult to explain. Then while the cannon was being stolen, he and Falstaff had been off playing Five-to-Two with the Hyos rather than tending to business. After that, choosing to fly with Falstaff again was going to be even harder to explain. It would be impossible to explain if they didn't get the cannon back.

If he tried to get into Alpha Wing, he'd never get to go after the cannon. There was no way to explain not shifting to Alpha. Ardr would never understand "security" as an explanation. He desperately needed some way to corroborate his judgment. So far everything was going against him.

He had spared a human trespasser, flown with the humans, taught the humans new tactics, and lost the cannon.

If he wanted to keep his land, he had to recoup his mistake in leaving the battlefield with those five porkies. So he had to stay with Pit Bull, and fly with Falstaff unarmed. And he'd have to explain why! *Reconnaissance, Intelligence, Security.* The words had no translation, but *traitor* did. Or, until now, he'd thought it did.

It was too much. Head pounding with tension, claws aching for a real kill, he flung himself into his sand bed and was astonished to find nearly eleven of his sixteen hours gone when he woke up.

He felt a little better until he noticed his message screen glowing. Falstaff had sent him a long, long text on security procedures and someone else had deposited a huge text on flying Reconnaissance. There was no end to it.

Everything in him rebelled. Studying humans had been a stimulating, intriguing adventure. But it wasn't fun anymore. He needed to go home. He needed to Walk.

He paced, raging, and then he threw a ration container against the bulkhead.

A few moments later the communicator signal shattered his eardrums. He screamed and slammed the instrument case with a kick that should have destroyed it. It chimed again. This time he triggered the accept, shouted "No!" and reached to break the connection.

"Commander!" complained Falstaff loudly. "Indiw?"

"What is it?"

"It suddenly occurred to me you might like to go to the gym for a good workout."

Indiw gazed at the scuffed bulkhead. Falstaff was just on the other side of it. Surely he'd heard the noise.

"Commander Indiw?"

"I do not believe your exercise facility can provide what I need at the moment. I am, however, grateful for your consideration." Stiff formality was the best he could offer.

"I hope you're not angry with me?"

"No," he snapped. Then he made a concerted effort to release his tension. "I have chosen to fly with you once more. I would not do that if I were angry with you."

"Well, no, I don't suppose. Thank you, Indiw. That's a big relief, and—uh—thank you."

There. It was done. Indiw broke the connection. He had to study. But first, he folded away the furniture and performed the complex exercise formulated to bring calm.

It was only partially effective, but he made it suffice. As soon as they recaptured the cannon, he could go home and run through his forest, go Walking, and forget everything he'd ever known of humans. *Everything*.

Meanwhile, he applied himself to the new texts. When he finished with the material they'd sent, he tried to get something on the mission they were to fly, but every effort was thoroughly balked by a screen that flashed ENTER SECURITY CLEARANCE CODE. He had just learned what one went through to get such a code, so he dropped the matter.

He had just donned a fresh flight suit and packed a small bag of necessities when a summons from Captain Lorton dropped into his hopper.

Indiw presented himself at Lorton's office hoping Lorton had realized Indiw was a fighter pilot not a photographer.

"Ah, Commander, please come in. Sit down. I won't offer you something to drink, but please consider yourself made welcome." Lorton folded himself down into his desk chair. He almost didn't fit, his legs were so long.

"I was on my way to check over my craft. I hope this won't take long." Indiw perched on the edge of his seat.

Lorton's mouth worked silently. Indiw deduced that he'd said something wrong again and the knowledge grated on raw nerves. He'd already spent more time among humans than ever before. Lorton would just have to do some of the adjusting. Indiw refused to apologize. He was not joining their pack, and he was not going to participate in their pack-binding ceremonies!

"Uh, yes, well, Commander Indiw, I wanted to tell you this personally because I didn't want you to get the wrong idea. The decision was not easily made." He stopped, staring down at his desk screen.

"Decision?" prompted Indiw after a long silence.

"Ah, yes. We've reviewed the flight recordings—all the recordings—from your fighter. I want to impress on you that we consider you the best pilot in Delta Wing—by far and away the best."

That wasn't unusual. Indiw was accustomed to being the best pilot in any group. Then he went cold all over. Humans awarded public honors to people they considered the best. That was how he'd gotten in trouble before. Gripping his chair arms with fingers and claws, he said, "Captain—"

"Let me finish. Commander, you're the senior pilot in Pit Bull Squadron, senior in fact to most of the other pilots with the wing. In the normal course of events, you'd be bumped up to Pit Bull One and given command of the squadron."

"I—"

"But we can't do that."

Indiw's hands relaxed, dragging his claws through the chair arm fabric as they retracted in relief.

"I'm sorry, Commander Indiw. The promotion, the rank, and the pay should be yours. You've more than earned them. But you just don't have the grasp of command protocols yet. I know it's awkward flying as Pit Bull Four, with a Lieutenant ahead of you, but the two of you make the best team I've ever seen in space or atmosphere. We don't want to break that team up, so as awkward as this is going to be, we've decided to leave you in the Four slot, and Falstaff as Three, bringing in Pilot Commander Rafe Pendalton as One and his wingman, Dimitre Gare, as Two. I'm sorry, Indiw."

"Was there, perhaps, a female officer involved in creating this decision?" That had been close!

Lorton shook his head. "No. Why would you ask that?"

Indiw rose. "Just curious. I have to go now, Captain Lorton. Thank you for your thoughtful kindness." He walked out feeling considerably better. His luck had turned. At last. If he could stay away from the human females, he'd make it through this all right.

Still, his knees were shaking as he walked toward the hangar deck, envisioning what his neighbors would say if they knew he'd been seriously considered for a position in which he'd have to give orders to humans. He'd never live it down.

All right. One last mission, recover or destroy the cannon, and resign with enough ammunition to clear his name.

His strength came back as he ran through his checklist. The craft was no longer a fighter. He wasn't sure what it was anymore. The weapons control targeting apparatus had been connected to a battery of recorders. If he sighted on anything, it would only be analyzed right down to its atoms.

Well, no, the craft hadn't been totally disarmed. He still had his energy cannon, and his shields were as good as ever. Without the bulky, massive ordnance, the fighter was much faster, more maneuverable, and it had greater range.

He levered himself into the cockpit, brought up the systems and the instructions the engineers had left, and explored the new capabilities. He was still at it, somewhat impressed, when launch control summoned Pit Bull Squadron.

He went down the chute after Falstaff and took position in the formation. This time, he'd even known where to go right after launch. Of course, he had an edge. The two new pilots had been his students, and they'd flown simulator together several times.

"This is Pit Bull One. Pit Bull Three, close up. Pit Bull Four, are you ready?"

Belatedly, Indiw flipped his transponder on and let it exchange status checks with One's command console. "Countdown complete. Let's go."

"Commander Indiw, I know you prefer less formality, but this squadron has a tradition to uphold. Okay?"

Fine with me, thought Indiw. *You go hold your tradition up to you-know-where!* Well, maybe a human wasn't anatomically capable of that. Intriguing thought.

"Pit Bull Four, do you copy?"

"No. Actually I just heard you."

Three human voices joined in hearty laughter. It sounded truly ominous and made Indiw's hide ripple.

"That's the spirit! Let's go, Pit Bull!"

Someone started a song and the others joined in as they kicked up past lightspeed and arrowed toward their search area. There wasn't any reason to believe the cannon was in their area. The Delta Wing squadrons were spread out to cover all possible destinations for the cannon. Someone would find it, but it might not be Indiw.

Stifling an urge to go his own way, Indiw stayed with the formation. He had told Falstaff he'd fly with him again. He had to do it because he'd announced his choice. But oh, he needed to get away from humans! If *Tacoma* had not moved away from Sinaha and toward the border to give Delta a head start to the search area, he might have taken a little side trip home before starting out for Hyos territory.

As soon as they settled into the long run to target, Falstaff came on their private band. "Indiw, are you just in a bad mood, or is something wrong? I know you should have been slotted as One—"

"I am very glad I was not. It would have been a first magnitude disaster even if I'd resigned instantly. I don't wish it to be known I was considered for such a position."

"Oh. I hadn't thought of that. I guess you're right. Your—um—neighbors would never understand."

"No. They wouldn't."

"But it didn't happen, so what's wrong?"

Indiw considered denying it, but of all the humans only Falstaff had any insight into his problems. Perhaps he might have a clue to a solution. "It is necessary that I have a personal hand in retrieving the weapon."

"But you do! That's what this mission is all about."

"But what if one of the other squadrons finds it? And even if we do find it, I won't be able to bring it back. We're supposed to return with nothing but targeting data for someone *else* to use to retrieve it."

"Wait, now, let me think this through." After a long pause Falstaff said, "No, I don't get it. Ardr do understand teamwork. Look at the way you folks fly, depending on each person to do his job. Lord, man, you've got a whole civilization based on specialists teaming up to solve complex problems. That weapon is one example.

This is another. Everyone does their job, so the whole team succeeds."

"I see that, but the problem is that *I* should not have chosen to fly a noncombat role, because I am a combat pilot. But if I did so choose, then I had to have a reason to think the weapon is where I've decided to look for it—I have to *defend* that choice in order to retain the respect for my judgment that is necessary if I am to hold my land. This morning, when I tried to query the computer, I couldn't even find out where we're going, and there was nothing from which to figure out where the Hyos have taken the cannon."

"Weapon, Indiw, weapon. We don't know what it is. You don't have any idea how it works, remember?"

"So I've been told."

"Shit, I'm sorry. I didn't mean to give you a hard time. I didn't realize what a mess you were in, and I should have. But all I could think about last night was that I was responsible for you keeping security, and what would happen to me if you didn't! And here you are starving for the data you need to make your choices and going crazy trying to live inside our little human boxes. You should have kicked me!"

Indiw almost laughed. "Take it on good authority, you do not want to be kicked by an Ardr. It would be the last experience of a very short life."

Falstaff laughed.

"Pit Bull Three, what are you two on about?"

"Just passing the time, Commander Pendalton."

"We go silent at the Hyos border."

"We know. No problem."

Pendalton's signal died away, and Indiw said privately to Falstaff, "There's nothing you could do to acquire the information I need. No action of yours has caused my predicament, and nothing you can do can remedy it."

"No. I chose to splash down in *your* swamp. If I hadn't, you wouldn't be here."

How could Indiw admit that he had in fact struck to kill when he'd first seen the unconscious human pilot?

"Listen, Indiw, when we get back, I want you to explain your whole problem to me as best you can. A lot of people on *Tacoma* owe me favors. You've got to give me a chance to help. After all, I got you into this. I owe you."

Human help was the last thing he wanted. "Later, I'll consider the options. But right now, here comes the border."

Right on cue, Pendalton ordered them to drop below lightspeed to take their bearings accurately and sweep the vicinity for Hyos. With the refit, their sensors reached three times as far as a fighter's. No sign of the enemy.

"This is Pit Bull One. Instrument check."

Transponders hummed and they ran through the countdown.

"Pit Bull Squadron, attention," said Pit Bull One. "It is my duty to remind you that we must not fire on any craft unless we can identify it as a swarm member, not settled Hyos. We're not here, this time, at the invitation of the settled Hyos. If any of us fires injudiciously, it could be a serious infringement of the treaty—which is strained enough already. Therefore, no one will arm weapons without my express order. Is that understood?"

Two human voices assented crisply.

"Pit Bull Four, is that understood?"

"Clearly understood, Pit Bull One."

Pendalton ordered them into enemy territory, silent running, stealth fields full on, power on minimum.

Pendalton seemed to relish giving orders. Perhaps Indiw had not understood the pack-bonding ceremony of orders and regulations. Perhaps there was a payoff in the giving of orders as essential to a human's existence as land was to an Ardr, and that's why they fought for the right with such passion. Passion? Could there be a connection between giving orders and sexual functions?

That subject kept him thoroughly engrossed until they neared their destination and Pendalton ordered them to spread out and disperse their probe missiles over the target system.

There were ten planets, the usual habitable one, two marginally useful ones, and two gas giant protostars. Canted to the ecliptic, a mineral-rich asteroid belt held a few chunks large enough to be planetoids.

Hyos installations were everywhere, defenses up and sizzling with energy, sensor traps, patrols, even a space station bristling with armament. This system was a fort.

Indiw had flown many missions into Hyos territory to destroy incipient swarms—always at the behest of the settled Hyos to whom swarmers were a nuisance. Swarming was not an act of aggression to Hyos, but an act of reproduction. Settled Hyos were glad to leave birth control to the First Tier Alliance.

Indiw had seen many Hyos worlds and stellar systems, but never anything like this. The Hyos were changing. Fast.

They stood off a good light-hour from the star and plucked information out of the Hyos waste-energy, then sent in their smallest probes and scanned, slice by slice, through the whole system. It took hours of tense work, all the more tedious because it was fully automated.

But Indiw watched the images come in, hoping against hope that he would be the one to find the cannon. And then he had it. He was sure he had it.

He pondered the images his probe delivered. He hadn't chosen to search here. Why should he be the one to find it? This couldn't be it. Then he remembered the trouble they'd had designing the cannon's camouflage net. The thing emitted a characteristic signature—yes! Oh, yes! Yes! Yes!

He nudged his craft up next to Pendalton and, on his tightest beam, said, "I've got it, Pit Bull One. No mistaking it. Let's get out of here before we get caught."

"There's no way you could know that. We aren't here to analyze the data, Commander Indiw, just to collect it. Continue scanning."

Aghast, Indiw said, "But I've got the location pinpointed. I can't risk being caught—I should at least download—"

"Commander, we have our orders. I know that's difficult for you to deal with, but right now you will return to your station and complete your scan—under radio silence!"

He knew he should set course for *Tacoma* and beam his data ahead in burst code. They carried the burst transmitter so they could get their data home no matter what.

He eased back into position and let the scan program continue, considering his options. If he abandoned the squadron and none of them made it back, the humans would never understand, even though he'd found the cannon. If he explained to Pendalton how he knew for certain that he'd gotten lucky—but no, that would be a break of security.

And he still had no idea how to explain why he'd flown this mission. He'd had no way of knowing it would be here.

"What's up, Indiw?"

It was Falstaff, nudging into Indiw's area and hailing him on their private band, narrowed to the barest whisper, but still against orders.

"I've found it, but Pendalton won't believe me. He says to continue scanning, but that increases the risk, and this data must get back safely."

"What are you going to do?" asked Falstaff.

The human had not assumed he would automatically follow the absurd order. Amazed, Indiw asked, "What would you do?"

"Follow orders. But I don't have your problems."

"If I leave, what will you do?"

"Stick with the squadron and follow orders." There was a pause. "I think."

"What do you think?" asked Pendalton. He had pulled his craft up close and caught their exchange.

"That Indiw can analyze the data. He's found the target, sir."

"Maybe, but we need complete data on the defenses if we're to get it back. Besides, I've never seen anything like this place before. Something's changed with the Hyos, and we need everything we can get. Finish the scans. We'll be out of here within the hour."

It took twice that.

The whole time, Indiw sat there *knowing* they had all they needed, *knowing* their danger increased exponentially by the minute, *knowing* he should have left. It was the kind of knowledge that came only from mature judgment, and he was certain of it. But he didn't act. And he didn't know why.

Eventually, Pendalton ordered them out. They faded back, regrouped, and drove for home, preparing to spit their data out ahead of them as soon as they got within range.

Indiw wondered if his staying had increased his chances of getting his data out because now at least he had company on the trip home. But he watched his instruments for sign of Hyos, prepared to bolt at the first hint of discovery.

He was not the least bit surprised when his monitor clicked over and revealed a swarm of Hyos approaching dead ahead, spread out with their deadly energy net deployed to drag the human ships sublight.

★
CHAPTER
FIVE
★

"OH. MY. GOD!" ROARED FALSTAFF, CAREENING INTO THE
drag net and disappearing from Indiw's screen.

Then Indiw hit the net. The instruments went crazy. The
controls jammed. Power fluctuated. Somehow he got a claw
onto the sublight shift and triggered the turnover.

Internal gravity spun in dizzying whirls, then cut out
cold. His restraints bit into his flight suit cutting off circulation. His attitude control program struggled to reorient
the craft now that it understood they were sublight.

Systems came back on-line showing two porkies converging on him, flanked by four single-seaters. He fired
his cannon and drove straight for them.

"Wait for me!" yelled Falstaff. "Indiw, where do you
think you're going—you got no ordnance!"

"Climb!" yelled Indiw, fairly sure the human would take
the suggestion. He did.

Then Indiw streaked between the two porkies, fired on
one of the single-seaters, pushing it aside. Falstaff fired on
another single-seater, whiting out its defensive screens. The
two Hyos crashed into one another, and Falstaff swooped
down to take position below and to Indiw's right, running
before the pursuing porkies. "They never learn, do they?"

"They will when the swarms start comparing notes."

Pit Bull One and Two fell in before Indiw. Pit Bull One
said, "Pit Bull Four, close up. The wing is flying rear guard

for Pit Bull. We're to get your data back to *Tacoma*, but there's no time for a transfer. Here's our new course."

Pit Bull One's course data flowed onto Indiw's screen. He spared it only a cursory glance and dumped it into his stacker while nervously scanning their surroundings. It rankled to leave a battlefield before the last shot, but Indiw agreed that what he carried would be worth it. Behind them, their pursuers were accosted by two squadrons. But it had been far too easy to slip away from the Hyos net. And there weren't enough Hyos back there. Where were the others?

"This is Pit Bull Four. I recommend extreme—"

"Silence, Four. Go to lightspeed on my signal. Now!"

Simultaneously Indiw saw it. "Falstaff, no! Abort!"

The lightspeed transition had almost taken hold when Indiw hit the abort. Falstaff's craft shimmered and re-formed on his screen—aborted in time. Pit Bull One and Two flared into a small sun that collapsed into a black hole.

He and Falstaff peeled off to either side to avoid the hazard, then rejoined on course away from the battle.

Falstaff made a strange, gargling sound that might have been human profanity, then asked weakly, "What happened?"

"Tensor field. We've got to clear it before going hyperlight. Watch the spectrum at twenty-two angstroms. See the flashing? They've spread millions of generators no bigger than grains of bed sand. Instruments can't see them because these are smaller than any the Hyos have used yet."

There was a long silence. "Dear God in Heaven, Indiw, you are *good*!"

"If that's praise, it's too soon. Look behind you. There they come."

"Hyos! Dozens of them. You *knew* they were up here!"

"Judged. There were too few laying back to greet us. The rest have to be guarding the edges of the tensor field."

"You've got the payload. Run for it, Commander. I'll cover your tail." Falstaff fell back.

In the split instant he had to make the choice, Indiw saw the vivid image of the elder Falstaff sliced in half, lying tangled in a heap of corpses on the bridge of the old *Tacoma*. A dead hero. Then he saw the younger Falstaff beside him, blown to bloody bits. Another dead hero.

No.

With savage blows of his hands and feet on the controls, Indiw slewed around and aimed to join Falstaff at the point where he'd meet the first of the Hyos.

"Indiw, get *out* of here!"

"Is that an order, Lieutenant?"

"Oh, shit!"

"Your uncle had a policy. Never volunteer."

Falstaff performed a perfect loop and leveled out on their original course, pushing the refitted fighter to its new top speed. Indiw clung as if tethered and leveled out, redlining his drivers as he fought to keep up with Falstaff.

Oddly, the Hyos slowed, hesitating. Were they sorely puzzled perhaps by the atypical behavior of these two craft?

"I don't understand you, Indiw."

"I don't understand you, Ray."

Falstaff laughed. "Doesn't interfere with our flying."

"So maybe it doesn't matter."

"What matters is we've got no ordnance!"

The gap between them and their pursuers opened steadily as they approached the edge of the deadly field. If they could go to lightspeed—

"Commander Indiw, do you see what I see?"

Indiw's attention snapped back to the forward view. Four Hyos porkies. The pursuers hadn't been confused.

Even his new circuit design didn't have the range to give enough warning at the refitted fighter's new top speed. The approaching porkies were the last thing Indiw remembered.

Afterward, he pieced it together from fragments of impressions and Falstaff's remarks.

Their own speed had multiplied the impact of the porky missiles that hit them. The shields had no chance to respond at that speed. The pilot ejects, however, had worked.

Falstaff swore that Indiw had yelled "Eject!" whole seconds before the impact of the missiles their sensors had never seen. Most pilots never even remembered the eject system existed unless they were burning up in atmosphere. In space battle, the ejects were completely useless. They weren't fast enough, and the capsules were designed to be very conspicuous so rescuers could find them, but they didn't have much in the way of air supply or particle shielding. Thus, any pilot who ejected during battle would be destroyed by a negligent flick of the enemy's least weapon or, worse, left to fry in the radiation storm or suffocate.

So Indiw could not imagine himself ever trying it.

Thus it was some while before he could credit the half-fragmented memory of waking in deep space surrounded by nothing but a spinning panorama of stars.

His next solid memory was of utter darkness redolent of Hyos—an odor he'd become familiar with during the battle for *Tacoma* at Walter Falstaff's side.

Everything hurt. His hide was raw, his tissues bruised, his head pounding, his horns aching, and his eyes scratchy, his ears ringing, throat raw. He moved and his body expelled a grunt of pain that didn't even sound like him.

"Indiw?" came a hoarse whisper.

There was something wrong with his nose, too. That had sounded like Falstaff, but Indiw couldn't smell human.

Then he got a brief, acrid, choking odor and soft, moist skin brushed across his hide. Reflex jerked Indiw's hand up, claws out. He gripped the muscular forearm, just short of piercing the skin. Then he fell back, panting.

"Easy, guy," said Falstaff. "I think we're prisoners."

"Hyos don't take prisoners."

"Maybe these aren't Hyos? Maybe we've finally met up with another species? Or the Hyos have."

"No. They're Hyos all right. Just Hyos."

"How do you know?"

"Smell."

"Oh. I forgot. If you'll let go, I'll move back to the other side of the room. I stink."

Indiw pried his hand away from the human flesh. His arm flopped to his side like a lump of meat.

"You okay, Commander?"

Indiw ran a hand down his body, flexed his toe claws, and said, "No bones broken. I don't seem to be bleeding. My flight suit's gone."

"I'm naked as a jaybird, too."

Indiw made the monumental effort and sat up, propping himself against a wall. He was on the floor. Both wall and floor were slick but dry. The Hyos smell was strongest on the floor—perhaps they'd walked on it. Did Hyos ordinarily wear shoes? Who knew anything about Hyos?

"What is this place? How long have you been awake?"

"I don't know," answered Falstaff. "Humans would use a place like this for a meat locker. There're coils over there that seem like refrigerant coils, or dehumidifiers, or even heating coils, and I found preservation field nodes in the ceiling. There's a door with a large handle, but I can't budge it. The rest of the place is a featureless box. I just finished exploring when you woke up."

Indiw flashed on the image of the human handling his unconscious body. His claws flexed. Then he thought of the Hyos peeling him out of the flight suit and nearly vomited.

"Indiw?"

Indiw clutched his knees to his chest. "Yes?"

"I'm scared."

It sounded like a shocking discovery not a complaint. Indiw had spent years mastering suprasegmental phonemes of non-Ardr languages. The human was not asking for assistance. "Do you know where this meat locker is? What's around us?"

"No. Could be on a ship or a planet, or a station."

"I think a ship or maybe a station. Something large, but wholly artificial."

"How can you tell?"

"There isn't a hint of vegetation in the air. No dust. And there's some kind of very faint vibration in the deck, unmodulated, undamped. It could be deep underground, or some kind of surface habitat on an airless planet."

"I had no idea Ardr senses were so keen. It must be bloody painful to try to live on *Tacoma*."

"Unpleasant," allowed Indiw, "but not nearly as unpleasant as this. There's no air circulating in here."

"I don't think they'd haul us in from space just to suffocate us. I figured we'll make our break when they come to feed us. At least now you're awake, we'll have a chance."

Indiw hitched himself up, exploring his body's protests. "I'm not up to a fight yet. Besides, Hyos don't take prisoners. They may only want cadavers to dissect. They may be planning to let us die in here and then just turn on the refrigeration until they're ready to work on us."

"That's what I like. An optimist."

"If I understand the concept correctly, you'll never find an Ardr optimist. By human standards, most of us—the live adults anyway—are thoroughly paranoid."

Falstaff's flesh scraped against the far wall as the man slid down to sit on the floor. Indiw's horns sensed the outline of the warm body.

"You've perfected paranoia to a fine art. It's why we're alive now. You see threats where no human would. So far, you've been right every time. So assuming they don't intend to keep us alive, what do we do about that?"

"Do you know how Ardr young gain their first chance at a place in society?"

Falstaff's breath hissed in.

"I don't mean the killing of all challengers within the hatching ground. I mean the breaking out of the hatching ground. Of course, the gate latch is a puzzle designed to be solvable at a certain level of intelligence and maturity. But the rationale is simply that an Ardr who can be held prisoner is no Ardr at all."

"I begin to see your point. This isn't even a prison. It can't be as escape-proof as it seems. Do you suppose they're monitoring us?"

"No. If they'd planted monitors, there'd be fresher Hyos scent in here. But if it's a meat locker, it must have circuitry in the walls, the floor or ceiling. It must have a drain, and air circulation even if it's turned off now. It's a problem, a puzzle, not an obstacle. Perhaps the Hyos have set us an intelligence test. If so, then our best bet would be to ignore the obvious door and find another way out."

"Even if it's not a test, they'd be fools not to have posted guards outside the door. Indiw, I've been over every inch of this place. It's smooth. There's no other opening."

"Human, you have no claws and you can't smell—and I'm not too sure about your hearing either. I do not accept your examination as conclusive."

There was a long silence. "I guess that's a deserved insult. I don't really accept my observations as conclusive either, considering you're here. When do we start?"

Indiw was hungry, thirsty, shaking with exhaustion and pain, and thoroughly agitated by being confined with the human. The human couldn't be feeling any better—maybe worse. Never had Indiw been more motivated to achieve quick results. "We start now. Which way is the door?"

"To your right."

"The coils?"

"To your left."

"The ceiling height?"

"Has to be about eleven feet high. I can just brush it with my fingers when I jump. What I could feel of it is smooth like the walls, except for the preservation field nodes."

Indiw grunted onto his knees, then pushed up laboriously to stand. Congratulating himself on staying upright, he staggered toward the door. He found the handle with one outstretched claw.

The door was locked, of course, and might be bolted or barred on the outside. "No hinges. I think this is a pressure door. That would make sense on a space station."

"You're right." Falstaff's voice put him very close by.

"Ray, please, stay away from me." His claws ached.

The human backed off. "I'm sorry." Indiw smelled a burst of human fear. At least his nose was recovering.

"Give me room to work. We'll be out of here shortly. There'll be plenty of Hyos out there worth being afraid of."

Falstaff backed off, and Indiw turned his attention to the door. It was sealed by a single panel that slid across from his right to his left. He could feel the difference in the way it mated into the cowling on the left. He could also smell Hyos more strongly on the left. They habitually touched that wall—yes!

"I've found the control for opening the door from this side. It's covered by a flat panel, a faint crack outlining it. It won't open, but I think the door is powered, not mechanical, and controlled remotely. If they expect us to escape, they expect us to force the door open this way."

Satisfied, Indiw turned to search for alternatives. "The coils are on the back wall, then?"

"Right. You want me to move out of the way?"

"The door control is on the left about halfway up from the floor. Go see if you can open the panel while I check out the coils." Without claws, Falstaff probably couldn't force the panel, but then Indiw had learned not to underestimate humans. He steeled himself to pass the human in the confined space and pitched forward into the coils.

With his nose on them, he could smell the refrigerant. "Falstaff, this place could get very cold very fast."

"That's what I thought. Those coils are huge. Maybe they put sizzling hot meat in here."

"I've got enough problems without your imagination."

"Sorry. There's only one thing worse than being trapped in a small dark place all alone."

"And what's that?"

"Being trapped in a small dark place with someone of uncertain temper."

"I see your point." Indiw found a fitting that attached the coil to the wall. The contents of that coil would be lethal to both human and Ardr in such a small space. Without letting himself dwell on it, he used a claw to loosen two screws and gave a firm tug.

At the loud screech, Falstaff called, "What was that?"

"I pulled a coil off the wall. I think I've found our way out."

"Way out? What kind of a way?"

"I'm not sure. There's a conduit that carries air and water, a bundle of connectors to the coils, and a power cable, too. At least it feels like the power cable on the porky. I think that when this freezer is working, the conduit is closed off by a force screen that controls the air flows, sorting the incoming molecules by temperature and molecule type—maybe sterilizing, too. There's a faint stirring of air in the conduit—might lead to the ventilation system."

"The sealing field is off now?" Falstaff had come halfway back across the locker.

"Yes. Perhaps they forgot about that. I'm not sure the opening is large enough for your shoulders."

"They're flexible. I'll manage."

The human's shoulders did not seem all that flexible to Indiw, but what did he know? It would be a tight fit for both of them. Someone Lorton's size would never make it. And there was no telling where this conduit would lead. The door might be better. No time for second thoughts. "You can follow me in, but stay well clear of my feet. You haven't seen what my claws can do to human flesh."

"I hope I never do."

Indiw was half into the conduit, so the human's voice sounded oddly muted. He squirmed forward, got a claw hold, and pulled and pushed himself in, careful not to puncture any of the hoses, tubes, or cables that lined the conduit.

Three body lengths in, he smelled the human entering behind him. "Indiw, does this seem too easy to you?" whispered Falstaff, apparently as conscious as Indiw that the conduit would magnify and channel sound.

"The Hyos stripped us to leave us helpless. I nearly broke a claw on the screws. Would you rather stay in the locker? Try the door? I choose to chance this exit."

"Indiw, I've trusted you before and it worked out fine. We're on a roll."

Indiw squirmed eight more body lengths before he deciphered that idiom. Why did humans always think that chance events of the past formed a pattern that would inevitably persist into the future? Maybe it had something to do with the way they formed patterns out of random dots?

"Feel the vibration?" asked Falstaff.

"Feels like air pumps." Indiw had spent some crazed hours crawling through the access tunnels behind the walls of the old *Tacoma*. This was similar. "And there's light ahead—faint—or out of spectrum for me. What do you see?"

"Dim, reddish light."

They came out on a hanging catwalk above a tall, narrow crawlway. Large, rectangular conduits ran beneath the catwalk. Hyos odor was very, very faint—old and stale.

Indiw swung down onto the catwalk and reached back to help the human. They were both moving with stiffening agony. He hoped they wouldn't come to personal combat with Hyos.

Hesitantly, the human took his hand and swung down.

"There's enough space here. Better for you, too?"

"Lots. Which way?" asked Falstaff.

"Down, I think."

"Why?" Falstaff peered to his right.

"From the size of the air system, I think this is a space station. Find a hub, and we may find a port with a ship—to steal."

"Nice plan," said the human, looking down at his body. "But we need clothing first."

Then Indiw noticed the human's sex organ. He'd seen diagrams and pictures before, but the real thing was—interesting. Small wonder the human male felt vulnerable when unclothed. Their skin wasn't worth much as protection and their internal organs hung out without so much as protective fat or muscle—only a token haze of fur.

"If you have any suggestions," commented Indiw, turning to look for a ladder, "I'd be interested." He found one that swung down with a squeak. He descended with Falstaff right behind him. The skin of the human's buttocks was considerably paler than the rest of him. Perhaps it was a racial characteristic? Clearly the dark blotches scattered over the man's body were impact injuries, bruises. The areas with paler skin might be more susceptible to bruising.

Falstaff asked, "How about stealing some Hyos uniforms?"

"They wouldn't fit, and no Hyos would ever mistake us. And stealing them would be a risk."

"Hmm," said Falstaff, and fell silent.

"Our only hope is to secure a ship and be gone before they notice we're no longer in the meat locker."

"It's a long shot."

"Improbable? I agree."

Indiw led the way, but he only guessed they were in the space station he'd recorded, the very space station to which the cannon was tethered. It was at the central portion of the lowest part of the station. Of course, there was no reason to suppose Hyos used the same direction conventions in space that the First Tier had adopted. Why should they? He could be right next to the cannon or heading away from it.

Twice, they hid as parties of Hyos went by. They didn't seem agitated or purposive, so perhaps the escape hadn't been discovered yet.

"You really can smell them coming!" whispered Falstaff.

"Yes."

"Maybe we can get out of this."

"The odds are against it, but I'd rather die trying."

"There's a reason humans value optimism—"

"Shhh!" Indiw heard Hyos voices without smelling Hyos. Finally he located the source of the sound. He whispered, "On the other side of this bulkhead. Hyos. Hear them?"

Falstaff crept up to the paneling and pressed his ear to it beside Indiw's horns. He breathed, "I think we've found their launch control. I can't understand a word of it, but it has a certain cadence. I think they're expecting ships to come in soon. Maybe we're close to a landing bay?"

He had to tell him. He stared down the dimly lit access tunnel. No, the human would never go for it.

"What is it, Indiw?"

"If I'm right about where we are, the cannon is *that* way about two hundred meters." He explained the image that his sensors had drawn.

"I don't believe it."

"Neither do I, but nothing contradicts the theory."

"Indiw, it's a setup. Got to be. This is too easy."

"I don't know enough about Hyos to make that judgment. Well, what do you think we should do? Try to destroy the weapon—or just try to escape?"

"I hate to point this out, especially with how edgy all this has made you, but *you* outrank *me*, which means you give the orders and I follow them."

"You can't be serious."

He shrugged. "Just thought you ought to know."

Gripping all his self-control, Indiw whispered, "Falstaff, please tell me what you choose to do."

"Destroy the cannon."

Indiw nodded. "We'll do it together."

"Now that sounded almost optimistic."

"No. From what I know of the thing, it won't be easy to destroy. But perhaps we can render it useless to them."

"Sounds good. If it's that close, do you suppose we might find a laboratory set up to study it?"

"They haven't had it long enough to be set up to dissect it yet. For all they know, it could be trapped."

"Booby-trapped? Is it?"

"I don't know." It didn't seem likely.

"Great! Go to disarm it, and blow ourselves to atoms."

"I can avoid Ardr traps! Let's see what's up that tunnel there." It was a narrow crack leading off to the right. They had to turn sideways to shinny into it, pipes sliding coldly along their chests. In the narrow space, the pipes exuded a stench. Indiw said, "Sewage pipes, I think."

"Sometimes I'm glad I don't have your sense of smell."

"Sometimes I envy your lack thereof. Look, it opens out and the pipes get bigger. A recycling plant?"

"I smell it now. Can't be a high status area to work in. Dissecting a prize like that cannon has to have some status to it. We're going the wrong way."

"I don't know Hyos well enough to guess. Maybe they have different notions of status?" Truth Absolute, that humans had weird notions of same.

They inched closer to the place where myriads of large pipes converged on a large opening. "Indiw, I'm a pilot not a sanitary engineer. Let's get out of here."

"It is pretty ripe. Look, there's a hatch, pressure sealed."
It was the first one they'd found that looked as if it led out
of the maintenance tunnels. It had a handle not unlike that
on the door of the meat locker.

They squirmed up to it, Falstaff draping himself across
a large pipe to watch as Indiw examined the mechanism. It
was hard to say through the pervasive stench, but it didn't
seem any Hyos had been through there recently.

"Try it," urged Falstaff. "We're on a roll."

Humans also had odd notions of how luck operated. But
Indiw triggered the mechanism, and the hatch slid open.
The sewage plant was fully automated and deserted. As
the hatch opened, warm, moist air rolled out. To Indiw
the smell was so thick the odor had the impact of a solid wave of oily water. His throat closed, his horns protested. His lungs pulsed with pain, his stomach knotted
with cramps, and he curled into a tight ball, muscle locked
against muscle.

The next thing he knew, the hatch was shut, and Falstaff
was pulling at his limbs, whispering urgently, "Come on,
Indiw, let's get away from here! If that's poison—"

He could breathe now, but throat and tongue would not
function. He shook his head and pushed the human away.
At last he choked out, "Just bad, not poison."

Together they stumbled back the way they'd come, then
took another branch of the conduit system. Here, they had
to worm along on their bellies, and there was less light.
Indiw followed Falstaff's soft-bottomed feet, noticing the
toes and little symbolic claws were not like the older
Falstaff's.

The tunnel became taller and Falstaff stopped, sitting
up to wait for Indiw to draw up beside him. The human
said, "We could create a nice diversion by sabotaging that
sewage plant—or maybe just cutting one of those pipes."

"I'm not sure I'd want to do that even to a Hyos. After
all, these people aren't guilty of doing anything more than
what you or I would do at the first opportunity."

"Maybe it doesn't smell that bad to them, but it would
sure keep them busy awhile."

"Among humans, do the sanitary engineers usually turn out to search for felons?"

"That's a point. What do you think we should try next?"

He didn't want to point out how hopeless the situation seemed. All the human behavior manuals warned that ranking officers must not emphasize the negatives or it would destroy the motivation to win and Falstaff had already complained of his pessimism. It made no sense to Indiw, but he needed Falstaff's continued efforts.

Suddenly the human put both palms flat on the deck. "What's that? Indiw, is that what I think it is?"

Indiw leaned down to touch his horns to the deck. "Yes! Fighters returning to a landing bay!" He squeezed past Falstaff, scrambled a few body lengths, and again touched his horns to the deck. The signal was stronger. "This way!"

As long as the pulsating rhythm of landing followed by taxiing kept up, Indiw led toward the landing bay, squirming through narrow conduits, scrambling through flat tunnels where they had to worm along on knees and elbows. Finally, a conduit dumped them onto a catwalk strung above a deep, dark pit stinking of machinery. The catwalk gave access to the banks of gauges and dials hung from the ceiling.

The vibrations were very strong when he smelled Hyos. "Searchers. Coming this way," he whispered, motioning Falstaff to cover between two large pipes. He folded into a shadow. "I'll take the first one. You get the second."

"I haven't got any weapons!"

"That's all right. The Hyos will bring enough. Get down! Here they come." He hunkered into the shadows, glad his hide wasn't gleaming at the moment.

Indiw had no idea if this lighting impaired Hyos vision or aided it. He had no idea if the reddish-brown color of his hide would blend with shadow. But the white and pink human was clearly visible to him.

Two Hyos edged warily along the catwalk. They weren't in full battle armor, but they carried beam rifles and moved as if stalking in enemy territory. Indiw noted the extra joints in legs and arms, the elongated neck, and a lower jaw that seemed to be some sort of evolved mandible. Both

Hyos had pronounced bulbous bellies and sunken chests. He hadn't seen that on armored Hyos.

The Hyos stopped, scanning their surroundings. They'd heard or sensed or smelled something suspicious.

The moment the Hyos scent changed, Indiw sprang. With his right foot, he hooked the beamer out of the first Hyos's hands and sent it whirling in an arc toward Falstaff. He landed with a twist and rammed the claws of his right foot into the Hyos's soft midsection. Flesh gave with a warm, sensuous thrill. Thin purple blood erupted all over him.

Behind him, the sizzle of two beamers was followed by the stench of roasted Hyos.

Indiw gagged, held his breath against the reflex, horns throbbing with the vile odor. He folded over his misery. But inanely he noted the Hyos organs he'd exposed were no different from those of other Hyos he'd gutted.

Falstaff sidled along the catwalk, sweeping the beamer from side to side searching for another target. But there were no more Hyos. Without looking back, he motioned with one arm, urging Indiw up to join him.

Indiw heaved the two bodies off the catwalk, vaguely hoping to confuse their back trail, and grabbed the second beamer. He joined Falstaff, gratified that the human was almost as good as his uncle had been at hand-to-hand combat. Only now did he realize he'd forgotten to ask. Not all human pilots could have done what Falstaff had just done. He had to remember this was not the elder Falstaff.

When he caught up, Indiw whispered, "Nice job."

"I understand what you mean now—about being kicked by an Ardr. I'm impressed."

"The next ones we meet may be in full armor."

Falstaff flattened himself against the rail of the catwalk and gestured. "Is that another hatch?"

Indiw slithered past and examined the arch. He was so amazed he could discern fresh Hyos scent through the blood on him. "Yes. This is where those two came through."

"There are probably guards on the other side."

"Probably." Indiw moved along the catwalk and knelt to check the walk for spoor. He found fresh scent there, too.

Returning to Falstaff, he said, "Two more went that way. Try the guards, or two more searchers?"

"We must be near the engineering shops. If they're studying the cannon, the lab would be in this area."

Having been thoroughly lost on *Tacoma*, which was built to general First Tier specifications, Indiw knew just how useful their guesses were. "We've got to get an armed ship, blast the cannon, then get out of here. It's probably better to try to take the searchers and get down another level."

"They might have a set of scans and notes—maybe enough to reconstruct the thing for themselves. What's the use of taking out the weapon if we don't get the notes, too?"

"It's unlikely we'll get either, let alone both."

"Indiw, what have we got to lose? We're not going to get out of this alive anyway. So let's show the Hyos that one on one, they're outclassed."

Indiw had another one of those episodes where his mind simply and flatly refused to encompass the human's stated motivations. Then it came to him that a land holder fighting on two borders would also take wild chances, not truly expecting to win, but not willing to cede his land. He nodded. "The hatch, then."

Indiw worked the latch, and Falstaff held it so it wouldn't fly open. Dim orange light streamed from the slim opening. Falstaff fitted the muzzle of the rifle to the crack, angling toward the imaginary guard standing beside the hatch. Indiw crouched, nodding readiness. Falstaff fired.

Indiw slammed the hatch the rest of the way open and hurled himself through. As he fell on one of the Hyos guards, a rifle bolt scorched his head near a horn. The Hyos skull struck the deck with a loud thud.

Falstaff fired.

The stunned Hyos developed a smoking hole between the eyes. The other guard had a matching hole in his belly.

Indiw dragged one carcass back into the maintenance tunnel. Falstaff piled his Hyos on top and straightened to look at Indiw who was fingering his wound.

"You all right? That looks like it hurts."

"It will. Later. Let's go." The shot hadn't hit too near his horn or he'd be out of the fight just from the pain.

Peeking around the edge of the hatch, Indiw saw that the corridor was clear and quiet. It curved sharply in both directions. Obviously, they were near the bottom of the station. The docks had to be close by. But which way?

Falstaff said, "Let's try that door over there."

Indiw dashed across the corridor to the designated door. It wasn't a pressure door. It opened into a closet. Falstaff shrugged and took off along the corridor to try the next door. Indiw followed.

They had guessed right. Here were the engineering shops. Each room contained benches full of equipment in various stages of disassembly. Diagnostic instruments and boxed parts lined the walls.

The sixth door they tried opened to emit a vaguely familiar odor. He grabbed Falstaff's arm and dragged the human inside, closing the door.

"What is it? Smell someone coming?"

"No. I think it must be their 'night' cycle—if Hyos sleep at night." All the repair shops had been deserted. "There's something in here."

Indiw skirted a bench and moved away from the human, turning his head to catch the scent with his horns. It was illusive. Every whiff almost triggered a memory.

"*Pinhir!*" whispered Indiw, following a trail of scent.

"What?"

"Glue. *Pinhir*. It's a low temperature glue—look!" He ran to the bench across the back wall of the shop.

Falstaff raced after him. Indiw triumphantly picked up the targeting assembly and found the date and place of manufacture on the bottom. "This came from the weapon."

"How can you tell? It could be a piece of any fighter."

Indiw shoved the device at him, bottom up. "Manufactured on Tantigre Peak? Not likely."

"Then we've found it. I'll see if I can locate their data storage."

The lighting in the shop was also that odd shade of orange of the outer corridor, so Indiw couldn't tell the human what color coding to look for. In the porky he'd studied, the data storage modules had all been bright green—through Indiw's light-correcting visor, anyway.

While the human searched, he rummaged through the parts on the bench. Each one that was built of standard parts he tossed into a pile on the floor.

Two small items he didn't recognize, he set aside. With the rifle set on low power, he melted the pile into slag.

Falstaff returned to observe his handiwork. He was now wearing a loose smock with the sleeves rolled up. It seemed black with gray patterning, belted with a twist of wire. He looked odd with his knees bulging out below the hem. The garment barely concealed his external organs. "Well," said Falstaff, "that destroys the weapon. Does this look like a data holder?"

It was the right shape, but it looked black. "Could be." Indiw took the flat oblong. It felt the same as the one in the porky, though it was much larger and reeked of recent Hyos handling. "Where did you get it?"

"Out of that thing over there."

Indiw followed the gesture to a large dark display screen, hung above four consoles. One screen. Four sets of controls. He was glad he didn't have to learn to understand Hyos. Down near the deck, he found the slot Falstaff had taken the thing out of. It looked right. He searched and found three identical slots. He nearly broke a claw removing the protective grating, but then the modules slid right out.

"There might be a backup copy somewhere else."

"We can only destroy this machine and hope."

They jammed the muzzles of their rifles into the data slots and blasted. Then they broke the large screen and slagged the circuitry behind it.

Falstaff handed Indiw another loose smock and a twist of wire. "Here. Get dressed. We've got a long way to go yet."

Indiw took the garment. It stank of Hyos. He wanted to drop it onto a workbench, but it had pockets large enough to carry one of the data modules and the bits of circuitry he'd kept. Falstaff had the other two modules.

Cinching up the wire belt to secure the heavy objects close to his body, Indiw said, "Good. Let's go." He began rolling the long sleeves up. He'd have to watch out for Hyos reach.

Falstaff led the way to the door, saying, "Too bad we couldn't find something to eat."

"Who could eat in this atmosphere?"

"Me. I'm starved."

As they eased the door open, Indiw asked, "Do you think two fugitives would be able to steal a fighter on *Tacoma*?"

"I hope that was a rhetorical question."

Not really. "Corridor's clear. Let's go."

"Which way?"

"Pick one."

"That way."

Indiw went.

At the next intersection, Indiw sniffed Hyos coming toward them from the side corridor. Four Hyos. They had to be close to the landing bays, close to the ships that were refueled and ready to go, close to something to defend.

Indiw gestured the human back, held up four fingers, pointed to his rifle and then across the corridor to the other side. Falstaff nodded, hefted his rifle, and crouched.

Indiw leapt into the air, fired at the apex of his leap, and landed on the other side of the corridor mouth. He had downed one Hyos, but he hadn't made the kill. Falstaff darted his head and shoulders out of cover and squeezed off two shots. He snapped back as the Hyos returned fire, melting the corner of the wall where Falstaff hid.

Falstaff held up one finger, wetted it on his tongue, and scratched the air with the wet finger. Some good luck ritual, no doubt. Indiw broke cover, low, rolling over the deck and pausing in the prone position to fire off two shots, then continue the roll across the corridor.

He glimpsed two Hyos on the deck unmoving, and two crouched at either side of the corridor without cover. "I'll take the one on the left."

"Okay. On three. One, two, three."

Without warning, Falstaff charged firing steadily. Then Indiw understood three had been a signal. He broke for his Hyos, laying himself out flat in midair, fired, then tucked into a forward roll. The startled Hyos was right where Indiw expected. His left toe claws drank Hyos blood. Guts spilled satisfyingly.

Indiw came around to face Falstaff's opponent. But the human had taken care of the matter. Indiw straightened, examining the one he thought he'd wounded. No, killed. Good. He exchanged his depleted rifle for the guard's fresh one and acquired a knife, which he parked at his thigh by jamming its blade through the material of the smock. Falstaff did likewise. Indiw retrieved one of the items that had fallen from his smock and sealed the pocket.

"Which way now?" asked Falstaff, hitching his belt up.

"Backtrack the guards to what they were guarding."

"Sounds good. Maybe we should be Blood Hound Squadron."

Indiw looked at him blankly.

Falstaff grinned. "Just kidding. No offense."

Indiw had no energy to be puzzled. They trotted along the corridor. The human was sweating, though he professed to be cold. And he'd acquired a limp. Neither one of them was well, neither had much more of this in him. If those guards had come from a ready room, they were out of luck.

The Hyos scent swerved left. "This way." Another branch corridor, a short one, ending in closed doors.

"A lift?"

Indiw found the lighted display controls. He had worked for hours on the porky, but it hadn't had an elevator. And he was so tired. He stabbed at the control pads. Lights blinked. The doors opened. A lift cage. Probably.

Inside, they got the doors to close and open again, but the cage didn't move. Then, for no discernible reason, the doors snapped shut. When they opened again, bright yellow light hit them like a wall of lava. Hyos normal lighting?

And there before them lay rank upon rank of gleaming porkies surrounded by teams of busy Hyos.

★
CHAPTER
SIX
★

THEY HADN'T BEEN SPOTTED YET.

Falstaff said, "Still on a roll. But which porky do we try for?"

"Over there, in the far corner, by the entrance to the launch tubes. We want one ready to launch, so we take the closest." The launch tube was outlined in bright light and shimmered with a force field curtain across it.

"Way over there? Maybe we should try for another elevator closer to our target?"

"Sometimes your sense of humor leaves me cold." Indiw walked out of the elevator, rifle gripped for quick firing. His legs were shaking and weak.

Falstaff followed, muttering, "What sense of humor?"

They went fifteen strides before someone noticed them.

Then the Hyos erupted. Before the shouting crested, they pelted across the hard, cold deck. An object flew at them. Falstaff somersaulted and rolled under a porky. Indiw dodged the other way.

The flung object was a cutting torch spitting fire. It hit the deck and skidded after Indiw, its field taking a hunk out of the porky's support strut. Indiw grabbed the object, sliced through the strut, then took off.

The porky gracefully collapsed on three of his pursuers.

Falstaff zigzagged across an open space and dove behind

a wheeled cart piled with testing equipment. Indiw raked
Falstaff's pursuers with his beamer.

As Indiw caught up with him, Falstaff shoved the wheeled
cart at Indiw's pursuers. Together they scrambled under the
next line of porkies and ran down the next aisle. Ahead of
them loomed a double rank of unarmed Hyos. Behind them,
about twenty Hyos closed fast. Three of the lead Hyos had
rifles. One was in armor. Others in armor were converging
from all sides.

"This way!" yelled Falstaff and scrambled toward a porky
with an open hatch but no access ladder. He tossed his rifle
up before him and jumped to grab the cowling.

Indiw boosted the human through the hatch with both
hands on his muscular rump. A soft human arm reached
back and grabbed Indiw's arm right across the reflex nerves.
Indiw's claws extended, piercing human muscle. Then Indiw
rolled onto the porky's deck.

Falstaff pushed him toward the pilot's seat and struggled
to close the hatch while firing the rifle one-handed at the
pursuers. But the door was remoted to the pilot's station.
Probably.

Indiw skinned into the pilot's seat and stared at the
vaguely familiar controls, mind suddenly blank.

Falstaff yelled, "Close the goddamned door!"

When Indiw didn't move, the human dodged rifle fire
and screamed, "You *can* fly this contraption, can't you?"

It was fatigue, pure and simple.

"Indiw! Now or never!"

Indiw hit something at random.

Ignition roared and the craft lurched.

Falstaff grabbed the cowling and kept shooting.

Indiw managed to bring up gravity and close the door.
Falstaff sagged against the smoking bulkhead.

"Better strap into the rear gunner's seat. Here we go."

Indiw propelled the craft toward the exit archway in a
lurching, wandering course, experimenting with the controls though the Hyos might think it evasive maneuvers.
The porky probably had a launch program, but Indiw had
no idea how to boot it. Only once did he drag the porky's

keel across another porky. The clang-screech nearly deafened him.

Falstaff, gazing at the rear gunner's viewscreens, made inarticulate sounds of alarm and dismay at each course change. When they hit the other porky, Falstaff moaned.

Indiw remembered an article he'd read about what bad passengers human pilots make, and what bad patients human doctors make. He hadn't believed it until now.

"Hang on," advised Indiw and made for the archway. As they approached, dipping, pitching, yawing, Indiw thought the hole looked smaller instead of bigger. He didn't even know if the field was set to let them through.

A moment later, they hit the center of the field at a skewed angle. The porky bucked. Indiw fought the controls, scraping the deck. The force shield had not yielded to them, it had shattered. Behind them, the field collapsed to darkness and didn't reignite.

But they were not in the launch tube Indiw expected.

It was a space dock, sealed from vacuum by another sparkling field stretched across a very broad opening.

Beyond the opening, the cannon floated near the dock's rim.

What had appeared on his long-range scanners as a simple space tether now proved to be a tow line. The tow ship was parked on the dock near the force barrier, and the tow line penetrated the vacuum shield via a solid conduit.

It was the most nonsensical engineering Indiw had ever seen, but there was no time to admire the bizarreness.

The porky lurched under them. "Indiw, they're firing on us! Where the hell are we?"

"Space dock. Hang on!"

Indiw tried to align his craft toward the force barrier. If they hit it, it might shatter, too, decompressing the dock. On the other hand, it might be a lot stronger than their porky.

Indiw's seat jerked. Falstaff yelled, "Got him!"

Indiw twisted to see Falstaff had the rear gunner's position lit up. He'd fired something and hit something.

Indiw turned back just in time to see the deck fill his forward viewscreen, gyrating crazily.

When the crashing and crunching ended, Indiw hung by his knees from the seat dangling in midair. Falstaff knelt beneath him, reaching up for Indiw's arms. "Take it easy with those claws this time, will you?"

Blood still oozed down the human's arms. Indiw pulled his hands back. "Move out of the way, and I'll get down. Can we get out of here?"

"The hatch control is up there somewhere." He pointed at the pilot's console above them.

"Oh. Yes. Let me see if I can find it."

"What do you mean, find it?"

But Indiw didn't answer. He got a grip on his seat, unhooked his knees, and drew himself up to where he could get a knee onto the edge of the seat and reach for the control board. "There. Did the hatch open?" He dropped to the ceiling beside Falstaff and crawled toward the hatch.

It was jammed. But it wasn't against the dock.

Falstaff moved ahead of Indiw. "Look. Light! Push!"

They braced and put all their combined strength into moving the powered hatch by sheer muscle. The third time, it gave with a shriek, as if the mechanism had broken.

Outside, the air was filled with the sound of Hyos armor boots, dozens and dozens of them, converging.

Indiw hung and dropped from the door, and Falstaff passed the rifles down before following him. "Which way?" asked the human.

Indiw was completely disoriented. He turned in the general direction of the porky's nose and led the way.

As he came around the wreckage, he saw the tow ship ahead of them—very, very close ahead. They had missed it only by two porky lengths. "Let's try for that one!" said Indiw and charged across the open space.

Falstaff's rifle sizzled behind him. Indiw dove for cover behind the tow ship's rear strut. The spot his feet had vacated erupted in sparks. Peering out of hiding, Indiw found three armored Hyos converging on them, a fourth lying in their wake unmoving. Falstaff ran toward Indiw. Indiw aimed at the lead Hyos's neck, where a rifle could penetrate Hyos armor. The three Hyos were sweeping rifle

fire before them, forcing Falstaff to dodge wildly, but Indiw
waited for the right moment, then squeezed off a single
bolt.

The lead Hyos fell. The second had to jump over the
body. Falstaff arrived, passed Indiw, and streaked up the
ramp to the closed hatch of the tow ship. Indiw nailed
the leaping Hyos at the apex of his jump, and the third
Hyos went prone behind the dead bodies, aiming directly
at Indiw.

For one instant Indiw's scope showed the muzzle of the
Hyos's rifle. He fired. The Hyos's rifle exploded. Indiw ran
after Falstaff. The hatch was open. They tumbled through
together, and Indiw asked, "How did you do that?"

"We're still on a roll! Go for it, Indiw."

Indiw picked himself up and stumbled to the pilot's
seat. He stared numbly at the array of controls, unable
to believe they were identical to the porky's. There was
only one unfamiliar board. Falstaff fell into the copilot's
seat. "Hurry up, Indiw."

"How can you trust me after I just crashed that porky?"

"You didn't crash. They shot us down."

"Right." Indiw powered up the engines.

Something roared to life. On a long shot, he engaged the
automated routines and chose the first on the list. The tow
ship levitated, tucked itself up tight, and headed blithely for
the force screen. Indiw set half speed ahead.

They hit the force screen with a shudder. Alarms
screamed. The rearview showed the space dock force
barrier no longer glittered. As Indiw watched, several
Hyos bodies flew out, swept by escaping atmosphere.

Falstaff dragged Indiw's attention back to the forward
view. "My God! Indiw, it's monstrous!" They were heading
right for the cannon, and it filled the forward viewscreen.
"And we're attached to it!"

The unfamiliar board must be the towing apparatus. They
had to jettison the tow field. But how? He couldn't read
Hyos.

"Slow down, Indiw, that cannon has to mass three times
what this ship does. It'll tear us apart if—"

Indiw picked a likely looking touch pad and poked at it.

The displays all turned orange. Of course, without his light-correcting goggles, nothing looked right, but he could clearly see the change. He had no idea what it meant. Probably not a jettison. Maybe their own protective field?

A Hyos body smashed into the cannon, impaled on a projection, and floated grotesquely.

Frantically, Indiw tried to reduce their speed.

It did come down a bit, but then they hit the end of the tow field. The tow ship's internal gravity damped all but a bit of the momentum exchange. The cannon began to move.

"Jettison it!" urged Falstaff.

"I don't know how."

"We'll never outrun pursuers hauling a mass like that! Try anything you can think of."

"Look." Indiw pointed to the display that depicted the orange field englobing both the tow ship and the cannon. "I tried something at random and I think I secured the load so we can't lose it. I've no idea what will happen if I mess around with this now that the cannon's moving. It's right behind us! What if it crashes into us?"

Falstaff glanced at the rearview. Bodies and small objects had stopped blowing out of the space dock. Falstaff sighed. "Well, give it all the speed it's got."

"Got to pick a course first."

Falstaff looked worried. "I hope your astrogation is better than your helmsmanship."

"I only got to examine a stationary, derelict porky."

Falstaff dropped his face into his hands. The rolled sleeves of his smock were soaked with blood. He might have lost enough to be on the verge of passing out. Indiw wasn't even bleeding, and he felt weak himself. Behind them, the Hyos would certainly have scrambled their fighters.

He turned back to the boards in front of him. There had been something . . . oh, why wouldn't his brain work! One of the researchers on that porky had found something. It had made sense only because he'd known the Hyos astrogated in their territory using strings of beacons that summoned the ships along predetermined corridors. That was why it was so easy for a sortie of First Tier ships to get in and out of Hyos space without encountering civilians.

"I've got it!" breathed Indiw, seizing the controls. Moments later, he had a schematic diagram of local space with Hyos destinations and spacelanes marked in flashing colors.

Falstaff stared at it blankly. "Yeah, but what is it?"

On one edge of the schematic a line cut across the pattern of stars. "Oh!" said Falstaff.

Both pilots recognized the pattern formed by Hyos occupied systems near their own patrol territory, and both recognized the meandering path of the border. On the Hyos schematic, the other side of the border was dark, blank, and deserted except for one isolated point of light in a color different from anything else on the display. But there was no mistaking its location. Sinaha. It was connected to a point on the Hyos side of the border—a rendezvous? And that was connected to a moving symbol—the tow ship?

Indiw theorized, "This ship is probably a commercial vessel programmed to operate in Hyos space. They knew how big the cannon was—some Hyos must have surveyed it and escaped from the first battle with the data. To boost it off Sinaha and get it moving, they needed that cargo carrier. But it wasn't hefty enough to drag the cannon hyperlight. So this tow ship picked it up at this point here, and the program for the trip to Sinaha is still here."

Falstaff's eyes were closing. "If we can get back to that pickup point, we can yell for *Tacoma* to come get us."

"Not with this equipment, we can't."

"Bet we can, too. If I can just remember the damn code. They make us memorize it in basic training, but I haven't even thought about it for a couple of years."

Basic training. Indiw had never been exposed to the human's training. He had volunteered to fly with them the first time when *Tacoma* had picked him up after his base ship *Katukin* had been destroyed. They had assigned him a courtesy rank of Pilot Commander, issued him a flight suit, and sent him to fly with Pit Bull. There were a lot of things every human pilot knew that he'd never heard of.

He engaged the program to take them to the point where the tow ship had picked up the cannon and boosted the speed in steps. When they reached the end of the sublight speed range, he held his breath and stabbed at the control the humans had identified as the hyperlight transition signal.

A moment later he opened his eyes. They were still in one piece, and the screens had changed color again. He'd given up trying to name the Hyos colors. He had a crashing headache only partly from the lighting. The scorched streak on his skull throbbed madly.

For a few moments he watched the indicator moving along the track on the screen, trying to estimate their arrival time. They were indeed hyperlight, but going very slowly by fighter's standards.

"Come on, Falstaff, let's see if we can stop that bleeding."

Dumbly, Falstaff stared at his blood-soaked sleeves. He didn't seem to have what it took to move, so Indiw pulled him out of the seat and back into the crew's quarters.

The ship was compact. Three quarters of the space was blocked off behind hefty shielding for the engines. This ship was all muscle. But there was water from a tap. The Hyos idea of a bed seemed to be a round kettle-shaped ceramic pot to curl up in without benefit of padding. Neither human nor Ardr would fit, let alone be comfortable.

Indiw guided the rapidly wilting human to a spot on the floor near the water tap. They both drank thirstily using their cupped hands. Then Indiw had to help the human out of the smock. He didn't want to tear the thing off him since it was all there was to wear. The air wasn't warm enough for a human, especially an unclothed one.

The puncture marks from his claws were oozing. A couple of them were jagged slashes. As he worked at cleaning and binding them with strips torn from his own smock, Indiw asked, "You understand I didn't mean to do this to you?"

"Don't worry about it. Only scratches."

"Thoroughly septic scratches."

"Not likely to catch Hyos or Ardr diseases."

"Maybe not, but I've been around humans lately. *I* don't worry about catching human diseases!"

"The medics will fix me up when we get home." When the bleeding had stopped, Falstaff flexed his hands, then struggled up, saying, "Nice job. Now let me see to that burn on your head."

Indiw ducked his head away. "No!"

"You can't see it way up there."

"You get those hands of yours anywhere near my horns and we'll have another couple of inadvertent puncture wounds to deal with."

"Oh."

Then Indiw noticed the front of Falstaff's thigh. There was an ugly burn about a handspan down from the hip. Of course. The limp.

"Well, let's see what might be useful for burns." Indiw found a freezer with packets of what Hyos might consider food. Neither of them dared touch that, but there was ice. And in another small closet he found some liquid oil that didn't smell too bad, nor did it taste foul.

They tended their own burns and small wounds, and Indiw washed the crusted blood out of the sleeves of Falstaff's smock. He tried not to get the rest of it wet.

When he'd finished, he offered the remains of his own smock. "Here, put mine on, wrap the dry part of this one around your feet, and sleep. We probably have nearly two days before we get close enough to try signaling *Tacoma*— assuming it's still in the vicinity."

Falstaff shoved the smock back at Indiw who was squatting before him. "You'll freeze."

"It's not too cold for me."

Falstaff stared skeptically, still refusing the smock.

Indiw said, "Sleep. You've lost a lot of blood, and we have no food fit to eat."

Falstaff glanced about at the cramped crew cabin. "This must be getting to you pretty badly."

"I'll sleep up front. Just don't come up there to try to wake me or punctures will be the least of your problems." He rose to go. Falstaff stopped him.

"Indiw, when I grabbed your arm to help you up, I didn't mean it as a hostile move. It's a gymnastic move we learn in basic training. I didn't even think about it."

Indiw nodded in the human style. "I understood, but your grip triggered the reflex that extends my claws. A little higher or a little lower, and I'd have been able to control it. But not like that."

"I see. I'm sorry."

"Not so sorry as I. Yet here we are, alive and in possession of the cannon."

"It *is* kind of hard to believe."

"Then sleep and let the rest of your mind catch up."

Falstaff nodded and squirmed down as if luxuriating in pure comfort. Knowing what humans used for bedding, and well able to imagine how much the human was hurting, he had a fair idea of how much bravado had gone into the languorous move.

He went to stake out a place just behind the pilots' seats where, if he curled his knees a little to put his feet under the control board, he could almost fit himself onto the patch of floor. As far as he could tell from the plotting display, there was no sign of pursuit. But then they'd gone hyperlight very close to the stellar system, where particle detritus from the heavy traffic would obscure their exit.

Eventually, someone would figure out the only destination they could have aimed for. It might take a while with the disruption caused by the decompression. But surely there would be fighters ready somewhere in that stellar system. It was bristling with armament.

Then he began to think of it from another angle. Suppose Hyos internal politics slowed the launch of pursuit. This whole thing of cooperating swarms was new to them. It might not be so easy for them to call on others to chase their escaped prisoners. And then—maybe someone very high up in the hierarchy was embarrassed that some unlanded worker had taken live prisoners. That would account for the long delay that allowed them to escape unnoticed. Maybe they'd been arguing about what to do with the prisoners. And the escape, from the Hyos point of view, would be excruciatingly embarrassing to someone.

For that matter, how could the Hyos know that they didn't know how to astrogate this ship? First Tier fighters, like Hyos fighters, didn't stick to prescribed spacelanes. They might well expect the prisoners to try for home by some other route.

He fell asleep convincing himself they were safe, at least for a while.

And that was true. The pursuit didn't catch up with them until rescue approached.

Falstaff was weak, groggy, ill-coordinated, slow-witted, and Indiw thought perhaps a bit feverish. The wounds on his arms had developed an unhealthy redness.

But he'd wakened able to remember the code they needed to signal *Tacoma*. It was an ancient pulse code. All they had to do was put out a signal—even one carried on the Hyos communications channel—causing it to be interrupted in a certain nine-element pattern.

Or they could use the tow ship's own engine burping in that code pattern. Or even a simple light pulse signal.

If they'd been approaching an Ardr carrier, they'd have needed nothing more sophisticated than that either, but the code would have been more complex. Ardr ships, like human ones, monitored Hyos emissions on all frequencies, even occasionally deciphering their battle plans, though the Hyos used coded transmissions as the First Tier ships did. He was certain Ardr communications workers knew to look for the human pulse code. And surely there was one used by the Fornak, too, though Indiw had never worked with a member of the third of the three species that formed the First Tier Alliance.

Indiw was able to find the communications wiring, to set up a simple make/break switch on one of the boards. Falstaff sat in the pilot's seat tapping out the code as they approached the end of their programmed course.

There was no way for them to know if *Tacoma* had heard

them, or even if it was anywhere in the area. Even though they tried to aim the transmission at Sinaha, they knew they were wildly conspicuous to any Hyos around.

It was a nerve-wracking twelve hours later before anything happened. Falstaff, bleary-eyed, half lying on the pilots' console, one wrist propped in the other hand to ease the ache of long hours of tapping out the code, suddenly called out, "Indiw!"

Indiw had done six hours of code tapping already and was sitting against the wall in the crew's quarters struggling not to think about what a cramped space he was occupying with another creature who was not, repeat not, available as food. Soon he would have to trade places with Falstaff again. Falstaff's voice didn't register until the human called a second time, "Indiw! We've got company."

Indiw hauled himself to his feet and crept on shaking legs to the copilot's chair. He nearly blacked out from the movement, but then his vision cleared and he could see blips on the screen before Falstaff.

"Ours or enemy?" asked Indiw.

"I can't tell."

He tried working the viewscreens with his clumsy hands. He brought another direction into view. They both saw the second set of blips at the same time.

Falstaff said, "Oh, shit."

Indiw studied the board, too exhausted to be alarmed. "That group is closer," he observed, pointing to the first group Falstaff had spotted. "A lot closer. I think the other group is Hyos—we're reading their 'friendly' transponders at a much greater distance."

"I like your thinking. Must be human influence turning you into an optimist."

"Say that again sometime when I have the energy and I'll take you apart into your component cells."

"I'll bet you could. I'll mind my mouth."

"You do that."

The closer group finally resolved into a formation they both recognized. Human pilots. Several dozen fighters escorting four Search and Rescue. The lead fighters were flashing another code.

"What did they say?"

"I'll bet it says *Tacoma* but I can't think how to answer them."

"Vary your sending of the code you've been using."

"Yeah."

"Indiw, hold station. Here they come."

The lead fighters englobed the tug while the other fighters swerved around to square off against the incoming Hyos. They were, after all, in Hyos territory.

Search and Rescue then approached more slowly, and one of the white ships edged right up to their hull. There was a loud clang, and then a voice said tinnily, "Just speak normally and we'll be able to hear you. Who are you?"

Falstaff answered, sitting a little straighter, "Pilot Lieutenant Falstaff and Pilot Commander Indiw, Pit Bull Three and Four, reporting back to *Tacoma*. That thing behind us is the object we were sent to locate. We've got their research notes aboard, too. At least we think that's what we stole."

"They may be a bit annoyed with you. Can you follow us or do you need a tow?"

Falstaff looked at Indiw.

Indiw felt his hands shaking. A few days ago, he'd have been too proud to accept help. Now he shook his head in the human gesture of negation.

Falstaff said, "You'd better tow us. We got here on a programmed course, and we're not in such great shape."

"Need medical attention? Now?"

"It can wait. Take us home."

CHAPTER SEVEN

IT TOOK THE MEDICS THREE DAYS TO GET FALSTAFF
back on his feet.

Two hours after their return, the medics released Indiw
but issued him a vile-smelling disinfectant for his claws
and made him promise to scrub twice daily. Interestingly
enough, none of the humans blamed him for the accidental
clawing.

Grateful for his freedom, he sought his own place to eat
and complete his healing while *Tacoma* hauled the cannon
back to Sinaha. The engineers labored over the Hyos data
storage devices, the hand weapons, and the tow ship they'd
brought back. But Indiw had not informed them of the
cannon parts he had taken from the Hyos laboratory. With
Falstaff unconscious on arrival at *Tacoma*, there had been
no one else to tell them about the parts and no reason to
mention them.

By now the return of the cannon must have created
furious diplomatic activity at the highest level. He knew
that, among humans, pilots of his rank did not access such
information at will, even if they were personally curious.
He'd given up trying to understand why. Among Ardr,
even the youngest unlanded youth would have full access
to all information and an opportunity to contribute. How
else could they earn land?

A Pilot Commander, however, was expected to lay back

and rest while others took care of matters. At first, he was too exhausted physically and emotionally to do anything else. But within two days, he began searching *Tacoma's* information system trying to deduce what was going on.

On the morning of the third day, he learned that they had made orbit at Sinaha, and that a delegation of Ardr had arrived onboard to take charge of the cannon.

Still aching in every muscle and joint, Indiw performed a meticulous toilet, polishing his hide to a gloss that unfortunately highlighted the embarrassing bruises, dousing himself with scent eradicator, and dressing in his best set of land holder's straps and sandals. He had to admit he looked formidable despite the blemishes.

With the small cannon parts in a pouch slung from his hip strap, he went in search of the delegation. The highest status representatives of a planet would have to be met by the highest status person on the ship, and among humans that would be the highest ranking person, not the person with the appropriate skills. On *Tacoma* that meant the ship's Captain.

It would be wise if he made his first appearance while the delegation was still bemused by human hospitality. He needed to display his achievements before they discovered his shortcomings. Besides, there wasn't an Ardr on Sinaha who understood humans as well as he did. The conference was doomed if he didn't get there in time.

When he reached the deck where the Captain's offices were located, a guard in a crisp uniform saluted stiffly and barked, "Sir! The rest of your delegation is in room G-2. That way, sir. Our apologies if you've been inconvenienced. Sir."

Out of uniform, he wasn't recognizable to the humans. Interesting. Of course, it had taken him months to learn to distinguish humans and he still wasn't very good at it.

He found room G-2 easily enough. The trail of Ardr scent thickly laced with scent eradicator led directly to it. At his approach, the two guards on the door opened it and stood to attention to let him pass.

It was a large room with light adjusted somewhere

between human and Ardr requirements. Even the air was moving briskly and cool enough to breathe, though heavy with human scent. And they had politely refrained from setting out food and drink.

There the concessions to Ardr ended. The center of the room was taken up with a large, polished table inset with display screens at each place. The wall at the far end of the room was a huge display screen now showing Sinaha from orbit, portrayed in the most bizarre color scheme. There was no human awareness of how rude it was to flaunt one's ability to satisfy prurient curiosity of another's land and Walkways. The chairs at the table were adjustable to the three species of the First Tier, human, Ardr, and Fornak but they were set much too close together.

The delegation had spread themselves as far as they could from each other, but there were seven of them. The eight humans were jammed shoulder to shoulder at the end of the table near the large screen. The delegates must realize the humans had done their best to make them comfortable, which only made them feel guilty for their discomfort.

Indiw inserted himself into this scene as *Tacoma*'s Captain addressed the delegates, assuring them that there would be no delay in the return of the cannon, but explaining that some of the parts were missing.

Indiw chose a formidable-looking landed elder seated at the end of the table near him and stepped up behind her. She stiffened to show she would not attack and quietly he placed his bag of parts before her. He made significant eye contact, then retreated a half step behind her seat.

The Captain stopped speaking and assumed a politely inquiring posture, human style. He was of medium height, considerable girth, nicely cleaned off hornless skull, and pale eyes and eyebrows. His voice was deep-toned and smooth.

Falstaff stood up from among the humans. Beside him Captain Lorton snagged Falstaff's elbow just above the white bandages as if urging him to sit down. Falstaff's skin was blotchy, his eye sockets darkened. He did not carry himself with strength, but his voice was firm. "Captain Reid, may I present Indiw, the designer of our fighters' new circuitry." He sat down with not even a motion of the eyes to indicate that he knew Indiw in any other context.

Amazing. In front of the Ardr delegation, Falstaff had not identified Indiw's rank or squadron position as the elder Falstaff would have. He had used only the one achievement that had earned Indiw his land. A marvelous feeling washed through Indiw, as if he'd found a worthy neighbor.

All the Ardr turned to inspect him again. It seemed none of them had recognized him.

Suddenly they stirred. Clearly word of his exploits among the humans had filtered back to Sinaha. They were dubious about occupying the same room with him. It was hard to read their scents because of the suppressant, but they must know he'd chosen to fly among the humans again, to teach them to use the new circuitry. They were skeptical of his sanity, unsure if he had betrayed all Ardr to the potential enemy humans. But perhaps knowledge of his aberrant behavior with respect to the human intruder was not widespread, for there was no real revulsion in any of them.

"The pouch," Indiw said loudly enough for the humans at the other end of the room to hear, "contains the only weapon parts that were not fabricated from stock items. The weapon can be made functional again in a short time."

The elder female hefted the pouch thoughtfully. She did not turn to look at Indiw, but she remained grave, as if this news provided no hope for the future. The others fidgeted nervously, digging claws into the table.

Indiw said for their benefit but with his eyes fixed on Captain Lorton, "Had I not been present on the mission to retrieve the weapon, these parts might have been destroyed—or abandoned to the Hyos—unrecognized by those sent to retrieve them. No other pilot flying from *Tacoma* would have been able to sort through the pile of components in which I found these. They were in a lab far from the weapon."

Motionless and absolutely silent, the Ardr digested that, but Indiw followed their reactions. Slowly, grudgingly, very, very grudgingly, they accepted that his choices of action had been valid, responsible choices, if somewhat unorthodox. But they retained the aura of a land holder standing against overwhelming challenge.

That was reasonable in the elder female. But of the others, three were not landed, and the other three were young and strong. This was serious.

Indiw asked, "Is there some reason the weapon can't be made functional?"

The elder female said, "When the Hyos took the cannon, they killed all those expert enough to rebuild it quickly."

She had spoken in the Tier Standard language the Captain had been using, so all the humans had understood. They stirred and Indiw caught a whiff of sudden despair though he wondered if the other Ardr in the room could read human reactions. He protested, "But surely with these parts, others can quickly learn—"

"But not quickly *enough*," she said fiercely.

Captain Reid said, "Pilot Commander Indiw, please take a place at the table and accept our apologies for not including you in this meeting from the beginning or you would have heard the news with the rest of us."

The humans all shifted leaving a vacant chair next to Falstaff. Indiw stepped back behind the elder female and stood at a polite distance from the others. He hadn't told the humans yet, but he had resigned from their company.

Reid pretended not to notice Indiw's asserted choice to stand. "The strategic situation has changed. When you left on the Reconnaissance mission, the newly refitted Fornak carrier *Int** had just been dispatched to relieve us here so *Tacoma* could proceed to Aberdeen, which is also under siege. The Fornak vessel was to defend Sinaha until the newly commissioned Ardr ship the—uh, oh, yes—the *Kinuha* could get here.

"As soon as the *Kinuha* was in position to defend Sinaha, the *Int** would take up position between Aberdeen and Sinaha, reinforcing this region of the border.

"But this morning we got word that *three* swarms have formed an alliance to take Sinaha, Aberdeen, and the proposed Fornak colony world they've named Thait*o, thus moving this border back into First Tier space. That would leave four other new colony worlds vulnerable to the Hyos."

There was a stirring among the humans, but Captain Reid waved them to silence. "Yes, I know Hyos swarms do *not* form alliances. But now for the second time since the Battle of Aberdeen in which the previous *Tacoma* was destroyed, they have allied. Worse, our analysts suspect that the Hyos have increased their intelligence-gathering activities tenfold. Hyos have had advance warning of our moves, which is why they've been so successful here lately. And now we've learned something that must not leave this room."

He glanced down the table at the Ardr. "This room is equipped with devices to prevent anyone outside it from listening. If any of this is mentioned outside this room, it is possible that spy devices might detect the words and convey them to the Hyos. It is imperative that no one who hears what I am about to tell you repeats it outside a secured environment. Are there any questions?"

The Ardr were silent, bursting with the scent of questions.

"Do I have your agreement that you will guard this information?"

The human forced each of the Ardr representatives, but not Indiw, to agree aloud, clearly having learned of Indiw's difficulty with the concept of *Security* and knowing that an Ardr could only be bound by his own announced choice.

Obviously, Reid had no idea how offensive his demands were to the Ardr, especially when he passed over Indiw. They didn't know Indiw had signed the oath or what it would mean.

Trained diplomats, the Ardr kept their claws in and spoke impassively. But they had no understanding of why Reid felt so driven to denigrate them, and were too busy suppressing the urge to gut him to think it through. All they knew was that Reid held them in contempt.

Then Reid leaned both hands on the table, arms stiff, and said, "The *Int** has been captured by the Hyos. If they use it the way they attempted to use the old *Tacoma,* their Breeder ship will be aboard *Int*.* They will use the carrier to slip the Breeder ship through the planetary defenses and release it into atmosphere. According to the First Tier treaty with the Hyos, once that Breeder ship is on the ground, the whole planet belongs to them.

"*Int** is still heading in this direction, running silent of course. What the Hyos aboard do not know is that the new identification transponders on the *Int** are producing the code which has told us of the capture. They also do not know that *Kinuha* has been launched ahead of schedule and is en route to defend Aberdeen while we stay to guard Sinaha.

"*Tacoma* has seen continuous combat for sixty-eight days now. The *Int** is the same class as *Tacoma* and is newly refitted and supplied. Despite resupply, we are not at full strength. If it comes to a slugfest between *Tacoma* and *Int**—if the Hyos aboard know how to use that ship— *Tacoma* may not win.

"As I understand it, that cannon you have developed would be capable of frying a carrier's circuits even through maximum shielding. If that's the case, we need that cannon operational before *Int** arrives. Nine days at the outside."

"It's not possible," said the elder female.

From the odor of defeat, the other Ardr agreed. But their despair was so mixed with offense and suppressed rage that none of them was working on the problem Reid thought they were considering.

Indiw said, "I think it might be possible."

All eyes turned to him.

"We have the crucial parts. There are a lot of people who've followed the developmental work as I have. I'm going to try. I expect I'll have all the help I need."

Captain Reid looked at Captain Lorton. Captain Lorton looked at Falstaff. Falstaff scratched his nose nervously, scrubbed his face with one hand, then stood up again. It seemed he was not permitted to speak while seated.

"A point of information on Ardr custom, Captain Reid."

"That's why we invited you here, Lieutenant," said Reid.

"It is often unwise to attempt to mix human decision processes with Ardr processes. It would be a good idea to adjourn this meeting until tomorrow while Sinaha and *Tacoma* each draw up a plan for dealing with the *Int** problem. Tomorrow perhaps we can blend the two plans into a cooperative strategy." He sat down.

Captain Reid considered that, face contorted into severe lines and shadows. With many hesitations to choose his words carefully, he said, "This meeting was called to discuss returning the weapon to the planet's surface, and we have not yet accomplished that. If there is any chance that it could be recommissioned in time, it would seem that it is urgent to work out those transport details. Then we will adjourn to plan how to handle *Int** when it arrives."

It was obvious to Indiw that the humans were having some sort of dire difficulty, and the Ardr, already driven to the limit even for diplomats, now thought Reid had decided not to carry out *Tacoma*'s contracted defense of the planet.

The humans were behaving with the same inarticulate confusion he'd seen when they couldn't get their orders to flow through the proper channels. Though he couldn't see exactly where the problem was this time, he decided it was up to him to sort things out for both sides before they had a major interspecies incident.

He began by stating what was obvious to all the Ardr. "There's no reason to return the cannon to the surface. No land holder on Sinaha will allow the cannon to be brought to ground because the best way to defeat *Int** is to trap it between *Tacoma* and the cannon. If the cannon's on the ground, even on the mountain, that would bring the battle too close to our holdings."

Then he tried to explain the humans to the Ardr. "It might be necessary to meet tomorrow because both human and Ardr might not devise identical plans for trapping *Int**. They're not all in possession of all the information. For example, they don't know the cannon was designed to be installed on Tasmset. The mechanism will be easier to repair in vacuum, and it will work even more efficiently.

Some of the equipment is already on the asteroid. The asteroid's orbital position will be perfect for the trap, and if *Int** pulverizes Tasmset, it's no loss since it's nobody's land."

He ended serenely, "So all that remains is to work up a method of luring *Int** into position and a way for us all to coordinate our efforts."

He was certain he'd solved the problem but the humans were still hiding some sort of distress. The Ardr, however, had begun to think rationally, and Indiw felt them slide into agreement with him. That was a heady elixir indeed.

Captain Reid said, "Pilot Commander Indiw—"

"Oh," added Indiw, "I forgot to mention. I resign." He asked the Ardr female, "Could I ride down with you? There is so much to be done."

He retrieved the bag of parts as the Ardr rose. They were eager to get away from the humans who were still radiating mysterious distress. The elder female said in the local Sinaha dialect, "There's room on our craft. It seems you've learned some obscure things about humans, though your methods are—original. I wouldn't have been able to settle the matter so neatly. I'd like to hear your reasoning."

It was wonderful to be accepted. For the first time since he'd seen the young Falstaff's face, he was confident that his land was safely his to hold.

He went ahead and opened the door for the group and stood aside as they exited. But before he could follow, Falstaff cut him off. "Indiw, you can't leave now!"

"We only have nine days. That's—"

"We have to talk. You can't just say, 'I resign,' and walk away. You reenlisted for the duration of the emergency. If you just walk away from that promised commitment—that openly declared choice—you're going to create a monstrous incident. Captain Reid has a lot of problems with what you just did and said in this meeting—and you weren't even part of the planetary delegation, so you can't speak for Sinaha!"

"I'd have chosen to come if I'd known about it. I don't see what the problem is."

"That's exactly it. It's going to take a while to explain it to you and to figure out what to do about the mess. You can't just walk out now because you feel like it."

The Ardr delegation was waiting for him by the lift doors. They were all looking at him, but Falstaff had spoken softly enough that they wouldn't have overheard.

"Ray, I can't just sit around on *Tacoma* when I have work to do. Look, I arranged my own ride home this time, so no one would be upset. I admit, I should have told Records yesterday to take me off the payroll but I was too busy trying to find out what's going on. And it's a good thing I did find out because if I'd missed this meeting, there might have been a violation of the Articles of the First Tier Alliance. Now they're waiting for me. I have to go."

He began to turn away but Falstaff danced in front of him—carefully keeping his hands behind him. "What do you mean, violation of the Articles? Indiw, that could be damn serious! Come on, you've got to talk to Captain Reid about this or he's going to blow—"

"Serious? Is that all? Just serious?" The human obviously had no idea what had happened in that room. Could the Captain have been just as ignorant? He could, indeed. Indiw remembered the woman who had been *Tacoma*'s interspecies Protocol Officer and talked him into accepting the Croninwet Award in public ceremony. She wouldn't have let this happen. "I doubt there's any point in talking, and I have things to do. They aren't going to wait very much longer."

"Wait!" Falstaff danced in front again, stalling Indiw in the middle of the corridor. "An hour. That's all, just an hour. Then I'll fly you down to wherever you want to go. Come on, Indiw, after all we've been through together, surely you can spare me an hour. A personal favor?"

"An hour with Captain Reid?" He'd soaked up enough torture for one day.

"If you don't, it's likely tomorrow's meeting will be an even worse disaster than this one."

Indiw's imagination served up a vivid image of the conference room with human blood sprayed all over the walls, all because he didn't have an hour to talk to a human. "Wait here, I'll tell them I've got some things to finish and I'll be along soon."

He joined the group of Ardr and explained. They went on ahead, and Indiw returned to find Reid and Falstaff in front of the conference-room door. As he came up, Falstaff was saying, " . . . so I asked him to do me a personal favor. Captain, there's more here than—oh, Indiw." Falstaff moved aside to make room for Indiw.

Reid frowned. "Lieutenant, you are on duty, even though the Commander has—uh—chosen not to wear his uniform, you do not address a superior officer by his first name."

"That's what I mean, Captain! To Indiw, his name is the most respectful form of address. It isn't a name the way ours are—it's more of a title earned the hard way. And the title *Commander* is a far lesser one, to him an embarrassing one. When you called him Commander in front of his neighbors, you almost destroyed his effectiveness among them. There was nothing he could do but announce his resignation."

Reid made inarticulate sounds, then turned to frown at Indiw. "It seems we have more to talk about than I thought." He gestured to the door. "After you."

Indiw froze, responding to the gesture as if an Ardr had offered challenge. He stared at the lift doors trying to dispel the irrational response. "This isn't going to work. I'd better go."

"Indiw, don't—please," said Falstaff. "Come on, Captain. Indiw, we'll be waiting when you're ready." He urged the Captain back into the conference room.

He was on the verge of saying, *I've had too much of humans lately. I'm leaving. Now.* But then he thought of what it would be like if Sinaha were lost to the Hyos because he wouldn't talk to a human—who was, obviously, trying his best to reach across the vast gulf and talk to him. *A land holder does what he must to defend his land.*

He went in.

Falstaff, Reid, and Lorton were gathered at the far end of the table. Lorton and Falstaff were taking turns exhorting

Reid, but Indiw didn't catch the drift of it before they noticed him and stopped. Reid stood up. "Thank you—Indiw—I think we need your help more than we know."

"I thought I had resolved all the problems at the meeting. Apparently I have missed a few points myself."

"Let's see if goodwill can bridge the void between the stars."

An hour later Indiw had talked himself hoarse explaining how even diplomats had limits, and how his timely intervention had probably saved a couple of human lives. He'd explained twice, in different words, what the meeting had seemed like from his point of view. In the course of that, Falstaff hastily shut off the view of Sinaha which, they carefully explained, had been meant to be spiritually inspiring. So much for good intentions bridging the void.

Indiw learned that *Tacoma*'s current Protocol Officer had died in a kitchen accident when *Tacoma* had taken heavy fire from a swarm of porkies and some massive equipment had fallen on him. No replacement had yet been sent. His subordinates were experts on the Fornak, not the Ardr.

So it took a good deal of talking for the humans to grasp how big a disaster Indiw had averted. Finally, Reid said, "I can see now that we owe you our most profound gratitude."

Oh, please, no, not that! Indiw had had enough of human gratitude with the Croninwet Award. "I have done nothing that isn't necessary in the defense of my land. I have done nothing for *you*. I am not interested in being counted among you. I want nothing more than to go home and organize the cannon project."

Reid nodded, obviously stifling a mélange of emotional reactions. Falstaff was hurting, too. Lorton was confused.

Indiw added, "I don't think you understand what I mean."

Reid answered, "Probably not. It sounded—uh—I don't think you want to know what it sounded like. But if we're going to pull off a cooperative defense of Sinaha, you should understand where our problem is with your behavior, so you can try to head off any problems from the Ardr side."

Falstaff said, "It would be easy for the list of Indiw's misdemeanors to sound like—uh—censure."

Lorton said, "But we assume that you simply don't understand what we expect of a Pilot Commander."

Falstaff added, "Not that you're required to fulfill our expectations."

The two Captains looked at each other.

Falstaff observed, "Ardr are more intent on fulfilling their own expectations. That can be a very touchy subject—expectations—like orders and choice."

"Orders," said Indiw, thinking they'd finally gotten to what was bothering them. "I had the impression, during the meeting, that your chain of command wasn't working properly, but I couldn't figure out where the problem was."

Lorton shouted—*no, laughed,* thought Indiw. It was a huge, openmouthed burst of sound, like a sneeze that had caught him unaware.

Reid looked at him, and mirth burbled over into a roar.

Falstaff looked at Indiw, shook his head, and pressed one hand over his mouth.

Indiw waited warily, confusion mounting.

Finally Reid gestured to Falstaff and urged, "Tell him."

"The problem, Indiw, was you. You stepped outside the chain of command, forgetting or ignoring everything about going through channels. You virtually took charge of the meeting—which you hadn't even been invited to—and railroaded through a plan of your own devising."

"But I had the solution to the problem. What was I supposed to do, keep silent and let the Hyos take my land?"

"You were supposed to keep silent during the meeting and afterward *go through channels*. It's not your plan or what you said that got us all mad enough to kill—it's that you blurted it out in the midst of the meeting instead of going to Captain Lorton who would have taken the idea to Captain Reid and the other Wing Commanders. When you jump the chain of command, you get us all confused—just like we got your people too upset to think straight. See?"

"I think I do see. You regarded the meeting as a bonding ceremony to bring the Sinaha leadership into your group. But there is no such thing as a Sinaha leadership, not the way you mean it. And if there were, none of them would want any part of being a member of your group. It's the same mistake you keep making with me—you think that I'm Pit Bull Four, but I'm not. I just chose to fly on one or another mission to defend my land.

"The members of the delegation were all volunteers who thought they had enough experience of dealing with humans to cope with the cannon problem. But they'd never dealt with humans who weren't under the orders of a Protocol Officer, so your behavior irritated them too much. They thought this meeting was a problem-solving session with humans who were experts in handling massive cargo just as they were. But Captain Reid stood up and told them things having to do with tactics and diplomacy not cargo handling. Nobody else said anything, except to tell Captain Reid things.

"You thought you were making peace, and they thought you were trying to make war."

Reid gusted out a sigh. "Fine mess we made of it."

Indiw said, "It's not an irreparable mess." Then he tried a human-style smile. "Or should I talk to Captain Lorton and let him tell you what I said—*if* he decides to tell you at all, and if he can convey just what I meant?"

Reid returned the smile. "It does sound like a silly way of doing things when you put it like that. But how do your people know when to speak up—and when not to?"

"Those who can't learn that, don't live to adulthood."

"Ah—yes. Hmmm. So tell me how to fix this mess."

"Tomorrow, when a group comes up—it won't be the same people you met today!—to discuss how to set the trap for *Int**, introduce them to your tactical people, and the supply people, and the other experts involved in the logistics. Let each of the delegates choose to go with one of your people into the tracking room or whatever working area is involved and work out the details of the plan. You stay out of it, keep your command personnel out of it, and just let the experts talk to the experts in their own work areas—no meetings, no briefings, no formalities."

"But—but how would they all know they were working on the same plan?"

Indiw sighed. Maybe there was no hope. No. Falstaff could weave pattern. If one human can do it, then it's not humanness that's the problem, but just culture. Of course, there wasn't an Ardr alive who understood even one human culture.

Indiw said with the last shreds of his patience, "If you accept the plan I outlined, then you will all be talking about the same plan."

"How can you be so certain if they're all going to volunteer tonight—people who don't even know each other?"

"Because they're all my neighbors."

"You mean you know them all?"

"Of course not. There's a planet full of people down there. I only know a few hundred."

Falstaff spoke up. "Captain Reid, I think the answer is that those who wouldn't come up with the optimal solution to the problem wouldn't survive."

"No, no," objected Reid, "imposing uniformity stifles creativity, and that cannon is proof these people have their own creative geniuses."

At least *Falstaff* was beginning to understand. Indiw said, "Captain Reid, if you can't use my first suggestion, I have one other suggestion that might have an outside chance of success."

"I'm listening."

"Put Falstaff in charge. Don't give him any orders. Just let him do what he thinks is best. He proved to me on that Hyos space station that he has good judgment, and he can weave pattern. If he can prove to the delegation that he has good judgment, they may let him weave with them. Then he can give you the orders and your chain of command will work properly again."

The color faded from Falstaff's face. Reid's complexion darkened. Lorton dropped his face into his open palms. Indiw muttered, "Oh, shit. Not again."

"Indiw," said Falstaff softly, "I'm only a Lieutenant."

"But that can be changed, can't it?" He said to Reid, "Just make him a Captain or whatever rank is needed. He has the best skills for the job—"

"It's not quite that simple."

"Oh." He was so tired his horns throbbed.

After a number of false starts, Reid said, "Both of your suggestions have considerable merit, and I think they give me a good insight into the problem of interfacing with Sinaha's tactical experts. I can understand now why Captain Lorton was having such difficulty controlling you."

Captain Lorton was trying to control me?

Lorton spoke up. "Indiw, I knew there was no point trying to control you. I was trying to enlist your loyalty to Pit Bull Squadron, trying to show you a chance to advance your career. I was *that* close to slotting you as Pit Bull One, but now that I've seen what happens when you have command, I'm glad that I didn't put you up for it."

"He didn't mean that like it sounded," said Falstaff. "It's just that on the Hyos space station, you, since you were the ranking officer, exceeded orders. We were sent to gather data. We shouldn't have tried for the cannon."

"Imagine the current predicament if we didn't have the cannon—and its crucial parts!" said Indiw.

"Success," said Lorton, "isn't what counts!"

It isn't? The unsuccessful died bloody deaths in the hatchery at the claws of the successful. Very quietly, he asked, "What does count, then?"

Falstaff folded his hand tightly on the edge of the table. If an Ardr had done that, the claws would have bitten holes in the backs of the hands. He said, "I hate to tell you this, Indiw, but it's following orders that counts."

"Oh. I see." Ardr young had to claw their way out of the hatchery, surviving by strength and cunning, whereas human young survived by forming around the strongest leader and following orders—forming a pack. Of course. "I think our species may be irreconcilably different."

"Not as irreconcilably different as we both are from the Hyos," observed Reid without contradicting Indiw's fear.

"That's a point." The final war would not happen until

the Hyos were vanquished and that might be centuries. "I'll go home now and see if I can arrange that those who come tomorrow to work out the plan for the trap will be as tolerant as possible. I'll be back with someone to move the cannon into position as soon as I can arrange it." He rose.

Falstaff got up, too, and went with him toward the door, casting anxious glances over his shoulder at the two Captains. "I'd sure love to see how you 'arrange' it!"

"Your uncle didn't enjoy the few days he spent on *Katular* watching me arrange things. I haven't enjoyed the days I've spent here—fighting the inability to arrange things. I don't think you'd appreciate the work I must do this evening."

Falstaff stopped him at the door. "You're not supposed to just get up and walk out on a meeting with the brass. You're supposed to wait for them to dismiss you."

"I'm all out of patience waiting. I've done everything I can do. I just want to go home."

Falstaff's expression twisted into a mischievous grin so reminiscent of the elder Falstaff Indiw just stared. The human said, "Come on, make their day. Throw them a crisp salute. Go ahead. You know how. Come on, we'll do it together. On my call—break!"

In unison, they saluted the "brass."

Falstaff called, "I'll take him home, and be back as fast as I can."

And they were finally out of that dreadful room.

In the launch bay they found an orbital shuttle had been prepped for them and reserved in Falstaff's name on Lorton's orders. Falstaff delivered Indiw neatly to the public landing field reserved for offworlders' use.

As Indiw climbed out of the eight-seater's hatch, Falstaff stopped him. "I've got to ask you something. I really have to know. I can't just let this slide. Will you give me a straight answer?"

"If you give me a straight question."

"Pit Bull Squadron. It isn't really meaningless to you, is it?"

"It means a lot of things to me, but not the same things it does to you."

"What does it mean then?"

"A chance to defend my land."

"That's all?"

He knew Falstaff was thinking of his uncle's dying a hero of Pit Bull Squadron, as hundreds had before him, of the traditions reaching deep into the past symbolized by the missing man in the missing-man formation. He couldn't say that these things revolted him, though that was true. So he met Falstaff's gaze and said, "Is that *all*? There is nothing else besides the defense of my land."

After a very long time in which the human's brown eyes became filled with clear liquid that glittered in the lowering afternoon sun, Falstaff said, "Maybe I've never really understood that before. Thank you, Indiw. Thank you for explaining. I'm sorry if I've given you a hard time."

Indiw nodded, and started to turn away. But then he had one more thing he had to say. "Ray. I think I understand now what the squadron means to you. What it means may be different for you than for me, but the intensity of the meaning is the same. This time I've spent with *Tacoma* may cause me trouble for years to come, but I expect it'll be worth it. Getting to know you was part of that worth. Flying with Pit Bull was part of that worth."

The human stood braced in the hatch looking down.

Suddenly Indiw knew how to convey what he needed to say. "If you were Ardr, I'd choose you for a neighbor."

A grin split the young face. "And if you were human, I'd choose you for a friend."

Glancing about, nervous that someone might have heard the exchange, Indiw noted they were alone. He threw Falstaff a salute and said, "Pit Bull Four, out!"

And he left for home.

★
CHAPTER
EIGHT
★

EIGHT DAYS LATER INDIW WAS ON TASMSET INSTAL-
ling the last of the reconstructed circuits into the cannon
mechanism. As Falstaff would have put it, they were still
on a roll.

But Indiw was leery of how easily they had achieved the
long list of improbable feats. In his experience, a run of
favorable luck was followed by one gigantic disaster that
wiped out the gain. And he wasn't at all convinced that
the luck they were experiencing was indeed favorable. The
only bright spot was the limited human female involve-
ment. A human female Protocol Officer had talked him into
accepting the Croninwet Award, which had nearly cost him
everything. Since then, each unavoidable disaster in his life
had come from human female hands, mostly females with
benign intentions.

This project, however, was progressing astonishingly.
That first night home, Indiw had accessed the planetary
posting boards and listed his cannon project inviting all the
experts he would need. Then he had looked up the invitation
for representatives to design a plan for trapping *Int**.

To his delight, many of those who had volunteered were
ex-pilots he had flown with. He had entered his assessment of the qualities delegates would need to work with
the humans, appended a list of his experiences on which

he was basing that judgment, and outlined his plan for the trap.

Then he went for a Walk. He entered the Walkway after the customary hour so the lush woodland was deserted. The one female he sensed retreated instantly. His spirits plummeted. As he was about to leave, she returned with four others, judging his need to be that great. The five eager females ushered him into the largest immersion pool and kept him busy the rest of the night. It was a unique experience and one even his most popular neighbors had likely never known. Most females would gut a male for suggesting such a thing. And on the Walkway, landed females had the power of life and death. No sane male would cross an aroused female.

By the time he fell asleep, he realized why he'd been so short-tempered with the humans lately. Without quite noticing it, he had entered the phase of his life where he needed this even more than he needed to pilot his fighter and kill Hyos. He was landed. And now he was fertile, too. That's what they had sensed in him, a denied first fertility.

The next morning, after the most profound sleep he'd had since seeing the night sky light with signs of battle, he returned to his house and accessed the net. All the volunteer delegates who did not have the qualities he had listed had taken themselves off the list. Most had, however, contributed some brilliant twists to his plan. The delegation now consisted of eight Ardr who would weave perfectly— unlike the delegation that had gone to retrieve the cannon— and would be the most tolerant of the humans.

Furthermore, his cannon project had a full complement of talented technicians and cargo pilots. His judgment had been trusted. Body and mind flooding with exhilaration, he reached Tasmset to find that Ardr tow-ship pilots had nudged the cannon into an approach orbit to Tasmset, calculated to arrive by the time the cradle was ready.

Even as one triumph followed another, his work fell into a routine, giving Indiw time to brood over his inevitable fate when they discovered he'd allowed an intruder to leave his land alive. It spoiled his enjoyment of being accepted.

He distracted himself by using the superlative data access in the Tasmset residences to track the progress of the *Int** and follow the developing plans for the battle. Delta Wing had been flying Reconnaissance, but the results were under security wraps. What the humans didn't know was that every scrap of information they released to what they believed to be Ardr authority was put on the net for anyone to access—any Ardr to access.

Thus Indiw discovered that Falstaff was not flying with Delta Wing. He was working with the delegations from Sinaha to shape the defenses, working out the best deployment of the few spaceworthy craft Sinaha still possessed.

Eighty-two new fighters would be ready to fly by the deadline, but to find pilots they had to invite many of the older, retired pilots. To defend their land, of course they volunteered, but many were past the age of peak reflexes though at the age of peak judgment. Indiw was still at his physical peak, but it had been a year since his speed had increased. For the first time, he understood what it meant not to be good enough anymore.

And then he lost track of what was going on, for his own job became a series of harrowing trials. On the eighth day, six technicians worked round the clock to mate the components, energize the circuits, and test fire the cannon.

The humans had towed a derelict fighter downrange of the cannon. It was insulated like a carrier, and inside was an instrument designed to register the disruption the cannon was supposed to create.

The first two tries fizzled.

Indiw refused to check the data services, knowing that everyone would have a suggestion. The technicians met in the pressurized shack, removing helmets. Indiw wondered if this was the reversal of luck he'd been expecting.

The conference was short and savage, opinion divided on the cause of the misfire. They had barely half a day until the *Int** arrived. If Indiw hadn't known the cannon had fired successfully, he would have doubted the theory behind it.

The argument circled until someone, an unlanded youth, said from the back of the crowd, "On Tantigre, the power supply was regulated through Herzman coils—the kind the humans use. They installed the coils only a few days before the first attack. Do we have the same kind installed?"

People exchanged looks, some dumbfounded, others just confused. Twenty minutes later they agreed the problem had to be the irregularities in the power supply. The youth had taken a giant stride toward becoming landed, and he knew it.

"Indiw," said one of the older technicians, a female with lacquered horns and hugely muscled thighs that raised Indiw's juices, "do you suppose *Tacoma* carries spare coils? And could you talk them into selling some to us?"

Everyone turned to him. They did that when they needed something from the humans. It had become both flattering and alarming how much they trusted his knowledge of human ways. "*Tacoma* would rather *give* us coils than claw it out with the *Int**. Let me see if I can find the right person to talk to."

He left them grumbling that it was impossible to find a human able to choose, but if anyone could pull off that incredible feat soon enough, Indiw could.

Indiw returned to his place on Tasmset, daring to feel that if he could find the coils, even discovery of his aberrant behaviour wouldn't destroy his reputation.

For that reason, he contacted Falstaff first. He wanted it on record that Falstaff was the key to getting the coils, so if anyone challenged him about sparing Falstaff, he could point out that if not for Falstaff, Sinaha would be Hyos territory. Now, if only Ray could help. The elder Falstaff could have, but he had been a Commander not a Lieutenant.

To his surprise, Falstaff answered his call instantly. "Indiw! What the hell's the matter with that cannon? It is going to work, isn't it?"

"Maybe." He detailed their needs.

Falstaff frowned. "If we've got them, you'll have them. But why didn't you call Captain Reid?"

"Will he be insulted?"

"I doubt it. I was just curious."

"We've no time for curiosity. Fly the coils over to us as soon as you can. We may only make the schedule by minutes as it is." And he cut the connection.

Barely an hour later, Falstaff arrived in a cargo ship laden with every size and specification of Herzman coil that *Tacoma* stocked. "That resupply ship a couple months ago screwed up and brought us all kinds of coils we don't use. You've got pairs of everything in the catalogue. Take your pick." He brought a display reader into the pressure shack.

Three technicians and the youth who'd suggested the coils pored over the catalogue, the others grouped behind taking stabs at translating the human engineering specs.

Helmet under his arm, Falstaff stood beside Indiw and watched the group of Ardr, commenting, "I guess we're still on a roll."

"It makes me nervous when you say that."

"Wish I knew why. I'll try not to say it, though."

"I'd appreciate that."

They fell silent as the argument heated. Indiw watched with satisfaction. He had the right people here. Only the original builders could have done better. If Falstaff had brought the coil they needed, they'd succeed.

Eventually, Falstaff asked softly, "So that's how Ardr solve problems. Do you think they'll ever come to a conclusion?"

"Momentarily." Indiw understood his bewilderment.

Then Falstaff said a peculiar thing. "Looks more like a family quarrel than an engineering task force."

Thankfully no one heard him. They had reached consensus, and Indiw, noticing the satisfaction on certain faces, knew they had found what they needed. As the technicians sealed up for vacuum, Indiw led Falstaff out the airlock and set his helmet phones to speak privately to the human. "Advice: don't mention the word *family* around here. Let's go unload the coils so you can get back."

"But you're coming with me, aren't you? I brought your light-translating goggles and a flight suit made for you."

"Coming with you?"

"Wouldn't be a proper battle without Pit Bull Squadron."

"That's something else not to mention around here."

"Look, I'm sorry, I just assumed you'd fly with us so I had a fighter prepped and held for you. You're our best pilot, you know, and there are so many Ardr going to be fighting with us, we'll need somebody who can talk to them. Are you really needed here that much?"

Indiw watched the technicians triumphantly carrying off the crated coils. If this didn't work, he had no further ideas to throw into the pot. In fact, there wouldn't be time to try anything else.

If that happened, he'd be needed in space. And if it came down to it, he'd rather die in his fighter than here.

Seeing his hesitation, Falstaff added, "I meant that. You are the best pilot we have. I told Lorton I'd take the number four slot and he could put you into number three—or for that matter, I'd be glad to fly with you as number one but you'd quit cold if he tried promoting you. See? I didn't mention the two unmentionables."

After eight and a half grim days of strain, Indiw couldn't help but be buoyed up by Falstaff's good spirits. "I thought Delta Wing was Reconnaissance."

"We're back on combat duty as of noon today. Come on, Indiw, you'll need some sleep if you're going to fight tomorrow."

Indiw considered the choice.

Falstaff dangled another lure. "I made sure nobody—not maintenance or housekeeping or anybody—went into your quarters. It's just the way you left it. I know it's not home, but it's got to be better than what this asteroid can offer. A good night's sleep will help. Come with me, and tomorrow, if you decide to come back here for the battle, I'll run you over here early. Captain Lorton wouldn't argue about it— not anymore. He'd do anything to get you back."

"I resigned."

"Don't worry about it. They haven't put the forms through yet—you didn't sign anything, did you?"

"No." He was intensely tempted.

"Last I heard, they had you listed as seconded on temporary duty. You're getting combat flight pay for building this cannon!"

"Lorton does not like me."

"No, he just has a problem with your attitude toward orders. But he got a commendation for the wing's performance since we arrived at Sinaha, and he knows he wouldn't have without you. He's willing to put up with a little irritation when the results look that good on his record."

Falstaff's explanation of Lorton's motives suddenly brought back all the revulsion he'd felt when drowning in humans for so long. "Ray, I can't do this."

"Why not? Lorton's not a bad sort. He just never had to deal with Ardr before. I talked him out of putting you up for a decoration. I think I got him to understand how embarassing it could be for you with your own people."

"I didn't know you understood about that."

"Well." Falstaff's spacebooted toe drew designs on the rock. "You know I was the first recipient of the Walter G. Falstaff Scholarship, but you don't know that I found out where the scholarship fund came from. And after a good bit of study, I understood you had to get rid of the Croninwet prize money or remain unlanded. Establishing the scholarship was the most elegant solution. But that you named it after my uncle—" He looked up and their eyes met through two thicknesses of visor. "Don't worry, I've never told a living soul where the money came from, and I won't."

Indiw had *not* known who any of the Falstaff Scholars were, and he hadn't wanted to know. He hadn't wanted ever to be reminded of that episode again.

"If it hadn't been for the scholarship, I'd never have been able to spend all those hours on the pattern-weaving simulator. Saved our asses a couple times, no?"

"Not to mention the rest of our respective anatomies."

"Right. Look, if you'd rather fly with the Ardr, I can get your fighter stripped of the *Tacoma* paint job. Even in the morning, there'd still be time. But we need you out there tomorrow, wherever you choose to fly."

It was true. There weren't enough pilots.

"All right. Wait here. I'll tell the others."

The technicians barely looked up from the coil installation, unsurprised that he was leaving. They'd all expected him to fly. Why hadn't he seen it that way? Why had it taken a human to point it out to him?

They were halfway back to *Tacoma* before he admitted to himself that he was afraid. Now that his neighbors were so accepting of his expertise in human ways, he doubted he could remain uncontaminated. He didn't trust his own judgment.

As the landing bay deck came up to meet them, Indiw decided that, at the first opportunity, he would make public his doubts of his earlier evaluation of the humans as no threat. And with that, he felt better.

Lorton met them at the landing bay lift doors, a grin splitting his face. Hands self-consciously behind his back, the Captain gave an awkward but creditable bow of greeting. Indiw returned it and offered his hand for shaking.

"Captain Lorton, I believe I owe you an apology."

Lorton took his hand in a brief clasp and politely let go. "I can't see how. I haven't treated you too well in the past, but I'm acquiring an education. Welcome back to the wing, and I'll try to get on better with you this time."

In the lift, Indiw pursued the matter. "The last few days I was—uh—under your command, I behaved very badly." He couldn't stand between Lorton and Falstaff and explain how sexual frustration affected a landed male in his prime.

Falstaff leapt into the silence with an explanation. "No one can blame you for being a bit edgy. Any human in the same position would have been suffering from culture shock."

"That's one way to put it."

"Indiw, you had all the classic symptoms, and you even said it yourself—you couldn't stand to deal with the human way of thinking even one more minute. But you can now."

"It won't last."

"That's all right," said Lorton. "Tomorrow, these swarms will throw everything they've got at Sinaha, Aberdeen, and Thait*o. After we whip them, there won't be any more for a few years. I'll arrange to revert your status to retired. Don't worry, Falstaff talked me out of putting you in for a promotion to up your retirement pay, and if you're comfortable with that, that's the way it'll remain."

"I don't want any kind of promotion or recognition for any reason. I've already got all the problems I can manage."

"Fine. Now, tomorrow, Pit Bull will fly the left flank of the central formation. Falstaff, listen up. I've bumped you up to Pit Bull Two, and slid Indiw up to Pit Bull Three." Falstaff's jaw dropped. Lorton patted the air. "Twice already I've put a pair into the squadron ahead of you, and we've lost them. It's beginning to spook people into saying you can only survive flying in Pit Bull if you're better than the best or have some kind of initiation into the secret tradition or something. So this time, you're going to fly with Phips, and Indiw will pair with—"

"No!" said Indiw, putting a hand to the lift controls. The doors flew open. He didn't even check the deck number but stepped out. "In that case, I'll join an Ardr pattern." He began to stalk blindly down the corridor.

Lorton grabbed the lift door to prevent it from closing. "Commander Indiw, hear me out."

At the end of the corridor double doors led to a huge, gleaming kitchen where people worked amid steam and noise. Indiw paused, then took a few steps back to the lift rather than have Lorton shouting after him for the humans to hear.

"Delta Wing has been assigned to work next to the Ardr. I want to station Pit Bull between the Ardr and the formation. You and Falstaff will do liaison if something goes wrong. I don't have anyone else I can hand this job to." He swallowed hard and said, "Won't you help us out?"

Touched beyond words by the human's effort to span the void between species, Indiw returned to the lift but kept his hand on the door. "I'm willing to do the liaison job. But—

I can't explain why, but I won't fly with any other human than Falstaff." He had to justify letting Falstaff survive intruding on his land.

Knowing how human decision makers were trained never to change an order in front of a subordinate, he fully expected Lorton to stand by his decree. Instead, the man's face worked through a cascade of expressions ending with a cryptic grin. "All right, look. I'll put Falstaff and you as Three and Four, and Phips and Kleeg as One and Two. But I'm warning you, Falstaff, no more of this 'we're Pit Bull Squadron' stuff. If Phips and Kleeg don't make it, and you two survive again, we'll have a legend on our hands, and we don't need any more superstitions on this ship."

"Yes, sir!" said Falstaff.

"You'll do it like that, won't you, Indiw?" asked Lorton. He sounded as if his whole career depended on convincing Indiw to accept.

Considering, Indiw looked at Falstaff. He was chewing his lower lip. He didn't need to say anything. Indiw *knew* Falstaff wanted to fly with him—would have chosen to had he been Ardr and free to choose.

Indiw stepped close and leaned his shoulder against the lift door to hold it, lowering his voice to address only the two humans in the lift. "I do have another possible solution, if you'd like to hear it?"

Falstaff peered at Lorton. The Captain asked, "A solution to what?"

"Your problem with re-forming Pit Bull. Apparently Phips and Kleeg do not want to fly in the position which has gotten others killed?"

"Well, yes, but they will follow orders."

"I understand, but didn't the others you assigned as Pit Bull One and Two also express reluctance to fly with me?"

Lorton's expression went unreadable. Indiw nodded and continued, "Captain Lorton, why not assign Phips and Kleeg to be Five and Six to another squadron, and let Falstaff and I fly with the Ardr pattern?"

"The Ardr would never go for it! You don't know what we've been through with them these last few—"

"Put us on the launch schedule but don't assign us a position," suggested Indiw. "I'll see to it that we're where we need to be to perform the task we've accepted."

Falstaff's eyes were round and bright, eagerness quivering in every line of his body. His uncle had flown with Ardr, and was to date the only human who had.

When Lorton hesitated, Indiw said, "I don't respond well to taking orders during battle, and as you once pointed out, I'm not qualified to give orders. This solution sidesteps all the problems of my shortcomings and uses my strengths as well as Falstaff's unique accomplishments. Must you reject it simply because you didn't think of it first?"

"I'll let you know in the morning," said Lorton. "Fair enough? Muster at oh-five-hundred. Your orders will be waiting for you."

In the same tone, Indiw answered, "When I see what you suggest, I'll decide what to do. Fair enough?"

"Fair enough," agreed Lorton. Then he looked about as if only now noting where they were. "Excuse me, I can go through the kitchen. It's closer."

Indiw stepped aside and then found himself alone in the lift with Falstaff who keyed it back to the pilot's deck. "God, that was incredible, Indiw! I can die tomorrow with no regrets. I've lived to see it all!"

"Have you? I haven't."

"I didn't mean it like that! We're going to kick Hyos ass right out of this quadrant tomorrow."

"Of course."

"What's the matter?"

"Captain Lorton made a tremendous effort to reach out to me just now. I didn't make a sufficient effort in return."

"Lorton didn't make *such* a terrible effort. You negotiated from a position of strength, and probably won your point. Humans do that all the time. It's not an alien concept. That's how we do things in families and in business. It's just so—unexpected—in the Service. A Commander just doesn't negotiate his orders with the Captain who's supposed to be issuing them."

"I can't claim to understand that."

"You're just tired. When was the last time you slept?"
Indiw admitted, "I don't remember."

"Things will look better in the morning."

They didn't. The Hyos were early.

The scramble sirens went off at four-thirty. Lorton's
message in his message drop when he woke gave Indiw
all he'd asked for. Luckily, the previous evening he'd
arranged things with the two Ardr wings that had filled
in on *Tacoma*. They knew the mission he and Falstaff were
flying, and his assessment of Falstaff's skill at weaving
pattern.

Indiw's reputation had come a long way since he'd first
flown with the elder Falstaff. This time, Ardr pilots were
willing to accept them. And it hadn't taken days to arrange
it—only minutes. They trusted his judgment that much.

Or was it just that he and Falstaff were still "on a roll?"
He shuddered. If the dreaded disaster was due, it would
certainly arrive during the battle.

He met Falstaff in the corridor. The lift disgorged them
onto the teeming and bustling flight deck. The launch tubes
were all belching fighters into space in arrhythmic synco-
pation. Falstaff led the way to their fighters.

The paint jobs still showed the Pit Bull logo and the
Tacoma colors. "I prepped and checked out yours yester-
day," called Falstaff, giving his own fighter a once-over.
"Let me know if I missed anything."

He hadn't. Not only did everything check out, but the
fighter now carried its full complement of ordnance. Indiw
ran a hand over an unfamiliar green missile slung beneath
the carriage. "What's this?" he called to Falstaff.

"Porky buster. Damn things really work, too. You'll
see the control on your board. Use them like any seeker.
Guidance's based on that maneuver you invented—once it
acquires the porky, it waits and goes for the cannon port
when it blinks open. The buster got tested when they came
to pick us up—took no casualties. Been making them at top
speed ever since."

Indiw ran his hand over the slick paint reverently. "Sometimes human thinking is truly admirable." But they only had

four apiece. He produced his best imitation of a human grin. "Let's go kick ass."

Launch Control announced their wing. They launched behind the two fighters painted as Pit Bull One and Two, answered com-check as Three and Four, and then Lorton's voice said, "Pit Bull Three and Four, peel off and take your position. And good luck! Pit Bull One and Two join Hawk Squadron as ordered. Lorton, out."

The peculiarly reassuring cadence of humans organizing for battle fell behind as he and Falstaff, side by side, circled *Tacoma* to the launch bays from which the Ardr wing had issued. Indiw announced himself and had Falstaff speak so everyone would recognize the human. Then they took position outside the weave but moving in cadence with it. Falstaff never missed a beat.

Contact had already been made with the Hyos swarm at the edge of the stellar gravity well. The humans were fighting hard, but retreating as if losing territory to a superior force. It was part of the plan.

Tacoma's sensors had located *Int** at the protected heart of the swarm, with three huge fuel tankers and half a dozen wallowing cargo ships bearing everything the swarm needed to take up residence on Sinaha. Hyos swarms always carried their Breeder ship within a globe of fighters. They didn't care how many casualties the fighters took. The only thing that mattered to them was placing the Breeder in fresh territory.

The retreating humans were pulling the swarm into position where the cannon on Tasmset could range *Int**. But the angle of approach was slightly off from the predicted path. And the Hyos refused to be lured after the human fighters. The entire swarm swept relentlessly toward Sinaha.

Lorton's voice came clearly to Indiw on the private band. "Pit Bull Four, change in plan." Indiw's tactical display lit with a map of the battle overlaid with glyphs drawn in Lorton's assigned color. "See if you can get the Ardr wing to move to *here* and join with Alpha Wing to form a spearhead. We want the Hyos to believe your two wings are the major threat. Can you manage that?"

"Probably," agreed Indiw.

It took a moment to translate and send the tactical display and suggest that their best chance for success lay in creating the diversion the humans had concocted. It didn't take much to sell the idea. All the Ardr had chosen to lure the *Int** into the trap. Then they were streaking toward the swarm at full speed.

When they caught up with Alpha Wing, the Wing Commander introduced herself. "Captain Tagawa, Alpha Wing. Glad to have you with us. Commander Indiw, tell your people to take point. We go in through those porkies right there. Acknowledge." It looked like the strongest point in the Hyos globular formation.

Only then did Indiw remember Captain Tagawa from his brief glimpse of her down the table. Suddenly he was taken by a frisson of dread. But before he could say anything, the Ardr weave had focused on a clear weakness in the swarm's formation. This particular group of pilots had not flown together, nor had they specifically chosen each other. Half the pilots took off for the weak spot, the other half hanging back just long enough for Indiw to suggest Tagawa's idea.

Some of the remainder followed the broken-off weave, the rest moved ahead of Alpha Wing's attack-cone formation to provide the confusing point contact Tagawa had wanted. Indiw led Falstaff into that point weave, keeping them between the Ardr and the humans.

"Commander Indiw, you were ordered to take care of this! Get those pilots back here! Now!" Tagawa added a series of abusive curses officers were not supposed to use because it undermined some intangible called morale. It was a good thing the Ardr weren't monitoring her command frequency, or there'd be no hope of any of them staying.

Clearly, Tagawa was not like Lorton. And she was female. He tried to think of something diplomatic to say.

Falstaff muttered, "Here they come!" Indiw's tactical display blinked and produced Falstaff's mark identifying incoming Hyos.

The Hyos hadn't waited for the defenders to make contact. Their globe had expanded, as if someone had begun blowing up a balloon, and suddenly there were porkies everywhere.

"Break!" shouted one of the Ardr, and the weave melted and re-formed in a tight defensive stance.

Lost, Falstaff gasped.

Indiw snapped, "Climb!"

Two Ardr caught a porky in a crossfire. The porky exploded right where Falstaff had been. The weave danced and re-formed, advancing into the thick of the swarm. "Dive!" suggested Indiw. "We can take *that* porky." He highlighted the one he meant on his tactical, and Falstaff followed him down toward their target.

In the scant few seconds before engagement, Indiw explained to Tagawa, "The other half of our wing is targeting the fuel ships while we go for the cargo ships. They'll meet us in the center—and we'll need help then because *Int** will have a clear shot at us. If we can get *Int** to chase us, this will work."

"Commander Indiw, you're not in command here!"

"I know. Do what you choose. I'm busy."

Falstaff's first cannon shot jarred their porky out of position. Indiw added two hits of his own, swooped past, looped, and delivered two more smacks to porky shields as Falstaff pounded away in exact resonance from the other side.

The porky fired several times and missed, shaken by the pounding. Finally, Indiw got a fix on an opening port, and one of his smaller, ordinary missiles went home true.

The explosion threw them both away from the center, shields hardened to blinding white.

"Indiw! Port ninety, full speed!"

Indiw took Falstaff's suggestion. Before the porky on his tail could fire, one of Falstaff's porky busters took care of him.

They re-formed, and Indiw led Falstaff back into the weave, which had eaten a tunnel into the porkies nearly five layers deep. There were noticeably fewer Ardr now, but the humans had widened the tunnel behind them. They still had no sensor reading on the center of the swarm. The globe of Hyos ships was too thick.

Indiw addressed the Ardr, "The human objective is to
lure as many Hyos over to this side of the swarm as possible
so *Int** will have to move to stay in the center of the swarm.
We shouldn't penetrate too swiftly—give the rest of the
swarm time to react."

"That's a good point. Hyos are notoriously slow."

Someone on the front edge of the weave said, "Formation
of four monster-gunships approaching. Tighten. Break."

The weave shifted, and again Falstaff, flying far beyond
his weaving ability, lost the rhythm. Indiw had to lead him
to the edge of the weave where they picked out another
target, a pair of porkies accompanied by four fighters.

Indiw broke into Tagawa's band to inform her, "The Ardr
will slow now to give the Hyos time to pull reinforcements
over here." He didn't wait to hear Tagawa list his parents'
attributes but switched to Falstaff's band. "Ray, this is a
bad idea. There are too many of them."

One of the Hyos fighters flashed into a red ball of glowing debris. "That better?" asked Falstaff.

"Not much." A porky cannon shot smacked into Indiw's
shields, then he was playing tag with a missile that had
acquired him.

A strange human voice came through on the general band,
"Pit Bull Four, hold still and I'll pick that nit for you."

Indiw leveled out above the reference plane, and two
seconds later the missile blossomed behind him. He looped
high to weave a return to their chosen target. His tactical
display identified his rescuer. "Thank you, Hawk Four."

"Don't mention it. Need some help?"

Falstaff, slugging it out with one of the porkies while the
other took up position to pound him from the other side,
said, "Hawk Four, keep those fighters busy while we take
care of these porkies. Acknowledge."

"Acknowledged, Pit Bull Three. Here come my buddies."

Indiw, already lined up for a run at the porky Falstaff had
targeted, ignored the approaching humans and sighted on
the porky's cannon port. He came in at full speed, timing it
perfectly. "Break!" he yelled at Falstaff a split instant before
the target porky blew and bombarded the other attacking

porky with debris keeping it too busy to fire.

Falstaff climbed hard, heeling over to return while Indiw engaged the remaining, somewhat crippled porky in a slicer duel. Falstaff's shot went wild. Indiw's forward shield pulsed alarmingly. Falstaff streaked by, disappeared for a moment in a cloud of debris from a destroyed fighter, and came around in a perfect weave.

Indiw broke contact, dove under the reference plane, and wove to the other side of the porky. In three rhythmic moves, they had traded places, Falstaff drawing fire and Indiw taking aim at the porky's opening port.

Just as he fired, he took a hit from one of the Hyos fighters. His cannon shot hit Falstaff, whose screens pulsed and throbbed with overload. Falstaff yelled his indignation, wove to starboard, returned in pattern, and discovered Indiw slugging it out with the Hyos fighter, Hawk Squadron nowhere to be seen.

The porky laid down covering fire for his one remaining fighter escort. Indiw took another hit, his forward screen flashing to maximum and then blinking out completely.

"Shshshiiittt!" hissed Falstaff, seeing Indiw's plight. "Behind me!" he commanded.

Indiw took the suggestion, gluing himself to Falstaff's tail for the several seconds it took his beleaguered system to engage his backup shield. When it finally came on, it was weaker than it should have been.

Meanwhile, Falstaff had loosed a buster at the one remaining porky. Then, together, they wove around the lone fighter. Indiw scored just as Falstaff's buster went home.

"You were right," said Falstaff. "We needed help that time. Wonder what happened to the Hawks?"

They had drifted a considerable distance from the main battle zone. As they returned, Indiw scanned for the Hawk transponders, but they didn't answer. "Destroyed, I expect."

"Damn." There was real pain in his voice.

The Ardr and human wings were taking heavy casualties. The Hyos reinforcements had arrived. Retreat was cut off by a phalanx of Hyos. Their forward progress was blocked by an ever growing number of porky-fighter teams.

Indiw and Falstaff rejoined the shrunken human/Ardr force just as Tagawa was saying, " . . . heading 238, mark 5. And never mind what the Ardr do. There's no controlling them."

"Falstaff, what are they up to?"

"Trying to make it look like we're retreating. To force the swarm to travel toward the target range."

"From *here!*"

The half of the Ardr wing that had gone ahead to attack the fuel ships would be abandoned in the middle of the swarm. And if Indiw's group didn't go on, there'd be nobody in there to take out the cargo ships. Not one Ardr pilot would even consider that. This was where Indiw parted company with the humans.

To Falstaff and Tagawa, he said, "We're still going to try for penetration. See you back on *Tacoma*. Good luck, Falstaff." And he took off for the Ardr's maneuvering territory, joining the weave, which was once again in an aggressive battle stance. Four porkies had engaged the edge of the pattern at different points.

Indiw began to dance a kinkintash pattern as he approached the Ardr. The instant he made the first sharp turn, Falstaff's voice squawked in protest. The human had clung to his wake, and as Indiw turned unexpectedly, Falstaff nearly crashed into the Ardr fighter at the edge of the pattern. "What are you doing?" demanded Indiw. "You can't weave at this level. You belong with Tagawa."

"You're my wingman. We're Pit Bull Squadron."

"You have your orders from Tagawa. And you *can't* follow where I'm going."

In a small, odd-sounding voice, Falstaff said, "You really don't want me with you?"

"No!" He streaked away from Falstaff into the thick of the weave and picked up the pattern as the Ardr advanced into the heart of the swarm like a drill bit cutting into wood.

He told the Ardr what the humans planned. As he'd predicted, they all chose to keep on to their rendezvous with their neighbors at the heart of the swarm.

It was exhilarating to fly full out in the tightest, hardest kinkintash pattern a group of strangers could manage together. Two pattern repetitions and they were calling him by name. Three and he was ceded the drill bit point, the most difficult and dangerous position. He didn't mention his weak forward shield, but he favored it.

He danced to the death with two more porkies shorting out his slicer and going to backup, vanquished another with his third porky buster, and set up a pair of fighters to collide leaving debris that triggered the two missiles some Hyos had laid on his tail.

He lost his main tracking scope and went to auxiliary. His cannon was recharging too sluggishly. But the circuitry he had designed was solid.

He ceded his place to a fresh pilot and wove to the rear of the pattern, teamed with three other Ardr to knock off two skulking Hyos fighters, and wove into the center of the pattern for a rest.

They had long since lost sight of the humans. Finally, the resistance in front of them lessened. Indiw warned, "We could be very close to the heart of the swarm. If we break through, watch for *Int** to fire on us immediately."

The weave was so tight now that when a porky died on the edge of it, the shock wave almost knocked someone into Indiw's path. He had no choice but to hold position—any move he could make would throw four others into collision. The hapless one recovered, acknowledged Indiw's confidence in him, and wove back to the edge again.

Indiw continued his leg of the weave and emerged for another turn on point. At that moment, they broke into the hollow center of the enormous globular formation of the swarm. The empty space was a shock. Only their rear guard was still engaged in battle.

"Loosen. Break," suggested Indiw, when *Int** loomed on his tactical display. The pattern held but expanded the territory it occupied while everyone considered what weave would be most effective now.

"Scatter. Break," said someone else.

The whole pattern broke apart and Indiw dove straight down below the reference plane. In that same moment, *Int** fired. The carrier's huge weapon produced a cone of nuclear vibration that could disintegrate a fighter's hull if the shields failed. And they were just in range.

Indiw caught the edge of the field and felt his whole body tingle and go numb. But his tactical display registered the disintegration of several Hyos behind them.

His shields held. The cone died away. Recovered, he finished the scatter weave and re-formed with the other Ardr into the looser weave more appropriate to the open space at the heart of the swarm. As a unit now, they drove toward their target, the cargo ships, which were unarmed containers designed to land on a planet's surface carrying the maximum payload. The cargo ships' only protection now was a detail of Hyos fighters. These would not be the Hyos's finest. This was considered the safe post in the swarm's formation.

He had saved three slender missiles just for this job, and he took his place in the new pattern according to the ordnance he had left. If they could establish that they were the serious threat, *Int** would chase them and that would end it.

As they moved across the open space, Indiw scanned the battlefield. On the far side, he saw the remnants of the other half of the Ardr wing emerge from the wall of Hyos leaving a creditable hole behind them. Two broke away and aimed directly for the fuel ships where a cloud of Hyos fighters and porkies guzzled the matter-antimatter powder fuel.

As battle erupted over there, Indiw turned his attention to the rest of the battlefield.

The swarm's globular formation had indeed deformed as the humans planned. The opposite side had been thinned by Hyos departing for the diversion. Attacking humans had picked off solitary Hyos systematically until the Hyos had to contract their formation to cover one another. That placed *Int** off center within the hollow sphere. To compensate, *Int** moved toward the spot where Tagawa was still staging her diversion, pulling Hyos away from their formation.

Indiw looked closer. No, *Int** wasn't just compensating for being out of position. It was fleeing. "Here comes *Tacoma!*"

At that moment *Tacoma's* big guns let loose with all she had. *Int*'s* shields flared into scintillating tones of gold and copper. Ships that size normally had no maneuverability, but *Tacoma* had jettisoned all possible mass and personnel. The remaining crew were in pressure suits. The central tactical coordinators for the battle who usually worked from *Tacoma* had been deployed on other large ships. The humans considered their carrier expendable in this battle, though the Ardr didn't agree.

So while Alpha Wing and the Ardr pilots were mounting their diversion, *Tacoma* had circled *Int** to attack from the thinned side of the Hyos globe. And *Tacoma* moved so unexpectedly fast that the Hyos couldn't react. To them it must have seemed she came out of nowhere.

*Int** returned *Tacoma's* fire in kind.

The two ponderous behemoths slugged away at each other.

Tacoma, however, was winning. The globe of the Hyos formation was moving into the trap thinking they were deploying to fight *Tacoma.*

Satisfied, Indiw called out a pattern break, took his climb high above the reference plane, then dove down on the cargo ships leaving the rest of the pattern to deal with the few defenders.

He took a hit, tumbled out of control for a moment, recovered, then launched his missiles. Two struck, one went wild. The cargo ship broke apart into large chunks of debris expanding from a common center. Solid pieces slammed into his shields, alarms screamed at him, and something behind his seat sputtered. Large sections of his boards glowed with amber lights. He ignored them.

*Int** had changed course. It was now headed directly at the Ardr. All Indiw's instruments danced and flashed as the carrier sought to lock its smaller ordnance on the Ardr, but they were just beyond range.

"We've done it," Indiw announced. "Now run for your lives."

There was only one fuel ship left and all the Hyos fighters and porkies were grouped around it. The Ardr attacking the fuel ships heard Indiw's statement and saw *Int** coming. "Shukalar," said someone in the distant pattern. "Break."

"Shukalar," agreed Indiw, and took the first leg of that pattern to begin his group's weave. It wasn't much of a weave. The object was all possible forward speed without presenting a target for pursuit to acquire.

The two Ardr groups merged on an angle and headed for the wall of Hyos forming the thick side of the sphere. *Int** wallowed cautiously after, no doubt afraid to fire their big guns for fear of wiping out more of their own defenders. *Tacoma* pursued and kept *Int**'s shields bright and hard.

Apparently, the Hyos didn't yet know quite how to manage the carrier in a firefight.

Then, all of a sudden, the wall of Hyos before them parted. Someone exclaimed, "Why'd they do that?"

Indiw knew. "Scatter. Break." He let the current leg of his weave carry him away from the center of the pattern.

*Int** slicers flashed through the place where the Ardr had been just seconds before. Two Ardr did not take his advice and became rubble—which was what always happened to those who didn't have the judgment to trust those who had good judgment. He said, "*Int** can talk to its own fighters and we can't unscramble and listen. Shukalar. Break."

This time not one Ardr chose to do otherwise. Just moments after the slicer beams had dissipated, they bored down the hole the Hyos had left. The special tracker display that had been mounted on his board showed *Int** approaching the correct position.

Indiw was in the lead of the shukalar pattern now, so he was the first to see the remains of Alpha Wing ahead of them. He switched to the human band and said, "Pit Bull Four. Captain Tagawa, heads up. Here comes *Int**."

★
CHAPTER
NINE
★

THE FLEEING ARDR STREAKED TOWARD THE CONFUSION
of Hyos packed around Alpha Wing.

The humans had been surrounded, cut off, and their compact maneuvering domain was shrinking. That domain was
right on the target range of the Tasmset cannon. At the far
side, Falstaff was battling two fighters, his screens sizzling
green static, nailed in place by a Hyos slicer lock.

Tagawa's voice came through in a staccato rhythm direct-
ing the battle, but Indiw switched to the Ardr band and
said, "The humans are pinned down on the target range.
I'm going to break up the Hyos so the humans can move.
We've only got a few seconds until *Int** is in position."

He didn't wait to see if anyone agreed. The humans had
proven themselves valuable defenders of Sinaha. It would
be absurd not to help them. The war wasn't over yet and
they'd need all the help they could rally if more Hyos
attacked in the next few months.

Indiw switched back to Tagawa's band and suggested,
"Human pilots set course 512, 233, mark 8 and hold steady
at maximum speed no matter what we do in front or around
you. If you deviate from course, you'll probably hit one
of us."

Tagawa reclaimed her band. "Belay that order! Keep
tight formation and protect each other."

"It wasn't an order," corrected Indiw mildly. "Just a suggestion. Here we come."

The Ardr had decided Indiw had a good idea and followed him into the fray. He told them what he'd asked the humans to do. "But don't expect them all to do it."

There was just time after that for someone to mutter, "Maybe this isn't such a good idea. Can't trust humans to have the judgment they were hatched with," and then they'd engaged the enemy Hyos.

The humans were battle-weary and they'd been ordered to stay in tight formation, not to flee. It took them a while to decide that following orders would be suicide. Gradually, they broke off and assumed the recommended course out of there. Indiw, having established the Ardr in a battle stance, wove directly for Falstaff who was still trying to shake one fighter's slicer lock while dodging the other's cannon.

Doubly confused by the Ardr weaving and the sudden human mass movement, the Hyos began firing at every Ardr who passed. As usual, while they were swatting at a speeding Ardr, another would slide into position in the pattern and dispatch the bewildered Hyos. Indiw killed three that way without being directly engaged, and he set up another two for others to knock off.

Fireballs blossomed everywhere. Hyos fireballs. Indiw wove right through the glowing particle storms, his instruments impervious to the static, emerged, and picked off one Hyos who couldn't see him coming on whited-out instruments. Then he neared Falstaff.

"Pit Bull Three, need some help?"

"Indiw! What took so long?" There was a strained undertone in the human's voice. "Cut me loose and I'll tend to that bastard."

Indiw enabled his own slicer and dragged the knife blade of it through the field holding Falstaff to his attacker. The moment Falstaff was free of the slicer lock he took after the Hyos with the cannon.

Indiw dueled slicer to slicer for a few seconds. When he had the Hyos's screens fully engaged, defending against his slicing field, he switched all power to his cannon. The power diversion was much faster with his new circuitry.

The Hyos fighter flashed into an orange ball.

Falstaff's quarry retreated and he began to pursue. Indiw called, "Pit Bull Three, set course 512, 233, mark 8! Max it or you'll fry."

"Right!" agreed Falstaff and swooped onto the new course.

Gradually, the formation of humans emerged, reassembled in their usual relation to one another, all headed in the same direction, though some limped and faltered from damage. One was trailing fuel in a fine mist. The Ardr pattern formed around the steadily moving humans, and it had the effect Indiw had anticipated. None of the Hyos could figure out what to do. *Hyos never learn.*

They had just cleared the target range when all Indiw's screens turned to black and white snow.

The Tasmset cannon had fired.

But they caught only the edge of the effect. Indiw's backups took over and his boards produced mushy, fuzzy images in time for him to complete his next weave around Falstaff. Two other Ardr crisscrossed in front of Falstaff, and someone asked, "Did we get *Int**? My scan isn't clear."

Indiw's wasn't wonderful either, but his tap into the human command channels brought him a raucous human cheering, the chilling sound of the pack in triumph. "Yes. It's dead. But it's still coming this way on momentum."

And of course the only Hyos crew casualties would be those injured by exploding power transformers.

Right on cue, the three human boarding parties that had been lurking behind Tasmset converged on the lifeless carrier, grappled to the skin of the ship, and disgorged armored humans who cut their way through the carrier's skin. Atmosphere geysered outward carrying a few Hyos corpses.

The Hyos fighters and porkies not caught in the cannon's field finally understood they had lost their carrier. They fled. Within minutes, the battlefield was clean of Hyos.

Tagawa ordered, "Alpha Wing, tight formation, set course for *Tacoma.* Damage reports!"

As one, the Ardr pulled their maneuvering domain away from the humans' formation and broke into a loose, traveling weave, circling back to *Tacoma* pacing Alpha Wing. Indiw wove a strand that kept him on the side of the maneuvering domain next to the humans and at the forefront of the formation. Falstaff positioned himself at the edge of the human formation opposite Indiw's nearest approach.

Indiw listened to the Ardr discussing the battle. They'd lost about a third of their number, attributing that remarkable success to the porky busters, Indiw's innovations, and his work on the Tasmset cannon. His judgment was trusted now. Even his appalling lapse with the intruder on his land wouldn't now disenfranchise him.

Without warning, his com scanner flipped to Tagawa's band. "Pit Bull Four, report!"

"I'm here. What's the problem?"

" 'I'm here. What's the problem?' Is that how you answer your commanding officer?"

"Of course not. I don't have a commanding officer."

"The hell you don't!" she growled. "I'll have you up on charges for this day's work, mister, and insubordination will be the least of them."

If the two of them had been in the same room, Indiw knew he'd have gutted her with one kick and not cared about the consequences. In fact, considering his new position among his own people, he wouldn't even be inconvenienced for the deed. But it would be an embarrassing fit of temper not a judged act, he knew. People with her kind of faulty judgment didn't survive infancy among Ardr. So he had no experience dealing with such an adult.

Falstaff, flying on the forward edge of the human's formation, saved the moment. "Pit Bull Three here. Captain Tagawa, *Tacoma*'s broadcasting instructions."

As he spoke, the broadcast began to emerge against battlefield static and instrument damage.

" . . . repeat. There was no Breeder ship aboard *Int**, and analysis of debris has shown no sign of one aboard any of the cargo ships destroyed. The Breeder ship has yet to be locat—what? Oh . . . my . . . God!" There was a pregnant pause. "*Int** was a decoy! Repeat. *Int** was a decoy. The swarm's main force is approaching from the opposite side of the stellar system. The only force deployed over there is the Ardr's Gipper Wing."

Falstaff blurted, "Hyos will go through them like so much tissue paper!"

Indiw wondered how Falstaff had gotten such an absurd idea. The best of Sinaha's pilots were over there, a little slowed with age, but still the best. They'd eat a hole in the Hyos attack sphere. But only a small hole. There weren't enough of them. His foreboding had been more than justified. Disaster had arrived.

Falstaff muttered, "There goes our roll! Shit, Indiw, we crapped out, just like you said! Why do you always have to be right?"

Tacoma repeated the message and then another voice came on from *Tacoma*. "Captain Tagawa, take your remaining force and the Ardr and assume position *here*. Hold as long as you can as the Hyos globe passes over you."

Indiw's tactical display flashed, shifted color, steadied, and showed the Sinaha system graphically laid out with the new intrusion diagrammed. The new Hyos force seemed twice the size of the globe they'd just vanquished. *Tacoma* was organizing the scattered human forces to meet the Hyos on the side of the sun nearest Sinaha.

He also saw the positions and current trajectory of the other *Tacoma* fighting wings, and the elder Ardr fighters deployed to guard the far-side approach to Sinaha. Even as he watched, the other human wings re-formed, reversed course, and sped to the new battlefront. Red flashing points signaled the fighters too damaged to join the battle. They still headed directly for *Tacoma* or Sinaha.

The Ardr around him were getting the same tactical display and the announcement. Without exchanging a word except to name the new pattern and call the break, they reversed course and made all speed toward the new intruders. Only three of their number elected to head for *Tacoma* instead. Search and Rescue was already coming to meet those disabled craft. The pilots would be back in space if there was anything left flyable on *Tacoma*.

They pulled ahead of the human formation. It took a

while for Tagawa to issue all the necessary orders, to sort out who would go and who would return to *Tacoma* for repairs, and to re-form her squadrons.

In clear space, the Ardr pattern leveled out into straight line flight, in close order. Falstaff nosed up on Indiw's right and fell into the wingman's position. "Didn't think you'd ever fly a straight line!" he commented on their private band.

"Don't get too close. If Hyos attack, the break out of this pattern will be rather spectacular."

"I think all our Hyos went over there to join their main force."

"I think they're trying to land on Sinaha to test the planetary defenses."

"That's a chilling thought."

"No. Very few Hyos escaped us." Space around the *Int** was littered with derelict craft.

"Optimism?" asked Falstaff.

"Pragmatism. Not every landed Ardr is a pilot. And every Ardr, landed or not, has more combat experience than any of those Hyos."

"That's a good point. There's no such thing as an Ardr noncombatant." After that, they exchanged notes on damage they'd sustained. Indiw's forward shield was his most crippling problem. Like most of the others, he had several systems already on tertiary backup. But the whole battle had been fought in local space. He was low on missiles but had plenty of fuel for power and speed.

They were all tired, too. And the long, tense run across the stellar system was not restful even though they weren't attacked. It didn't last very long, either, for the Hyos swarm was speeding toward them, closing fast.

Watching the battle unfold at the edge of their detector range, Falstaff said privately, "I should have tried harder to talk the gippers out of this. I should have put them on atmosphere defense." There was true anguish in his tone.

"What do you mean?"

"The Gipper Wing. There was this one female—I think she's the oldest—who insisted they had to guard the far side of the system. I thought it sounded like a good, safe place to put them and let them feel they were contributing."

"This old female—did she have skin the color of dried human blood and horns tipped with gold ornaments?"

"That's the one. A voice like black velvet and a face made of vertical wrinkles."

"Never in my wildest moments would I dare to oppose her judgment in anything. It's always fatal. I wish I'd known she thought we needed a force over there. I wish everyone had known."

"Now, look, there's no way she could have known *Int** was a decoy."

"And there's no way I could have known it would be necessary to spare your life. Judgment doesn't work just on deduction. Judgment is the edge that an intelligent creature has against a hostile environment, and it comes from surviving. You only survive by doing the right thing without having *any* way to know in advance that it is right."

"No, Indiw. That's luck, not judgment."

"It's judgment when you do it on purpose." *Not as haphazardly as I do, trying to explain after the fact not before.* "Anyone who's lived as long as Uyitin has, does it on purpose. *That* is what deserves respect, not commander's stripes or captain's bars."

"You don't get to be a captain without having good judgment."

Loath to contest the point, Indiw said, "Mostly, maybe."

"Look, Tagawa's acting like an asshole. I don't know why. She doesn't have that reputation. You just ticked her off somehow."

"She has no confidence in her own judgment, so she has to rule by appeal to the force that stands behind her rather than by persuasion."

"There's no time for persuasion in battle."

Indiw touched his tactical display drawing a circle around the Ardr wing, which still held a long lead over the human formation. "You'll note that persuasion took much less time than orders."

"Because they each decided independently."

"And moved as a single entity."

"No way could that happen with humans."

"Exactly. Chilling thought, isn't it?"

"Isn't it." After a long silence, Falstaff added, "Indiw? Could I ask you a question?"

"Yes. Certainly. Why should you not ask?"

"I mean, this could be personal so maybe it's impolite or something. Bad judgment to ask an Ardr something that might seem like bad judgment, especially a landed Ardr."

"Ah. You've begun the journey to wisdom. I'm wearing flight boots. Ask."

Falstaff laughed, but there was a strain in the sound. "I was just wondering why you're letting me fly with you now. I mean—before—you acted like I'd done something stupid, betrayed your confidence in my piloting or something. Then you just took off with the Ardr as if I didn't exist."

"Ray, your piloting is better than your uncle's. It is a great joy to fly with you. You have done nothing but increase my admiration for you."

"Then why kick me in the gut like that? What did I do to deserve it?"

He owed him a straight answer even on the verge of battle—a battle against such overwhelming odds that it was certainly lost unless First Tier reinforcements arrived.

"Tagawa ordered your people to abandon my people—the segment of our wing that went after the fuel ships. In my judgment, their move seemed to be a solid judgment call. Every one of the Hyos who survived to flee is low on fuel, and that will help us. If a Breeder ship does get down, it may die without the supplies on the cargo ships we destroyed. *My* judgment required me to go after the cargo ships because I weave best with that group of pilots.

"But we could succeed only with the most sophisticated patterns—patterns we could fly only because those lacking judgment had been killed off and those with disharmonious judgment had gone for the fuel ships.

"I could not lead you through that weave without disrupting the wing. You don't have the skills. And I didn't dare risk it. Things are different now that we've flown the highest levels. They trust me more. That's why they helped me break Alpha Wing out of the Hyos siege."

"I wondered why you did that, too. Tagawa never said a civil word to you. I was shocked when you suggested I follow her orders. I thought you'd written me off."

"Since she's extremely angry with me, it would be bad judgment to get you in trouble with her. I may yet need the power your clean record gives you to get me out of the trouble my good judgment gets me into."

"So it would be bad judgment to waste my clean record?"

"Yes."

"You couldn't have thought that up in a split second."

"Judgment doesn't come from thought. Judgment comes from motivation."

"I don't think we mean the same things by those words."

"Probably not." Indiw's mind produced an image of the stars of Earth with lines drawn between them making pictures. "We don't classify things the same way. But we have two strong, basic motivations in common: to survive and to protect what is ours. You're good at surviving. And you're good at protecting. I'd still choose you as a neighbor."

"And I'd choose you for a friend because I trust your judgment. That's why I didn't follow you when you left me."

"Not because I outrank you and I gave you an order?"

"Well."

"I see."

His tone changed. "Indiw? Do you see what I see?"

Indiw's tactical showed Falstaff's pointer at the leading edge of the approaching Hyos. The Hyos were climbing out of the stellar gravity well up toward Sinaha while the *Tacoma* wings were accelerating downward to meet the globe.

Retreating before the Hyos, the Gipper Wing—Indiw wondered inanely what sort of ferocious pack hunter gippers might be—had created a vortex of chaos among the

Hyos fighters and porkies. Already, the Hyos were sending reinforcements to the challenged area, leaving other areas thinner.

Indiw saw immediately what the Ardr would choose to do. Tagawa would probably order her people to attack where the globe had thinned rather than wade in and support the Gipper Wing. He asked Falstaff, "What should I say to Tagawa to convince her to follow our lead in this?"

"What are you going to do?"

"Engulf the pattern the Gipper Wing has created and continue to bore to the center of that globe. The Breeder *must* be there."

"It didn't work last time. We almost got wiped out."

"But we achieved our objective, and you weren't wiped out."

"Tagawa will never go for it, not a second time."

Already the lead Ardr were exchanging commentaries with the Gipper Wing. The consensus was instantaneous. Indiw told Falstaff, "Slide in behind me, lock on to my tail and stick. When this pattern breaks, you and I will make a one-eighty at ten degrees below the reference plane, then a vertical climb followed by a dive at ten degrees, aiming for the point position. After that, it gets harder."

"I'm your shadow. Do we break left or right?"

"I don't know yet. Depends."

"On what?"

"What others decide. Quiet. I'm listening."

Uyitin's distinctively elderly voice called out pattern names and numbers of pilots needed to fly each pattern. It was a brilliant concept, and there was no trouble dividing their force to braid six patterns into one. Indiw volunteered himself and Falstaff as one unit of the simplest braid on the edge of the maneuvering territory.

As they approached the globe, some of the lead Hyos separated to come toward them. Someone breathed a soft "Primary break, now!"

Indiw told Falstaff, "Break left!"

They went down, then up, then down to the point. By the time they were in the new weave position, their pattern had become a long, hollow cone that swallowed the Gipper Wing whole.

The front end of the cone closed and the pattern braided into a swirling ball that rolled inexorably toward the center of the Hyos globe. Indiw led Falstaff on the outward leg of the weave, and they emerged on the surface of the ball approaching a very confused Hyos fighter standing almost stationary with respect to the globe's forward progress.

"Here comes our Hyos," warned Indiw. "You'll get one cannon shot, and I'll take him with the slicer. Okay?"

"Got it."

And that's exactly what they did. The bewildered Hyos flew apart into a thousand pieces. No explosion. He'd been almost out of fuel.

Falstaff fired on another Hyos, and Indiw gasped, "No!"

An Ardr swore luridly in two Ardr languages, cutting onto the human band as he spoke. Simultaneously he swerved out of pattern just in time to miss being blown apart by Falstaff's cannon shot, then had to emerge from the maneuvering territory to avoid colliding with another Ardr.

"Follow me!" urged Indiw. "And don't fire on every target you see."

"What did that guy say?"

"He said he'd take you swimming. You owe an apology."

"He'll get it. Look!"

The Ardr, outside the pattern and alone, was besieged by four porkies. "Let's go," said Falstaff and took off across the pattern.

It was sheer chance Falstaff didn't collide with someone, but it seemed nobody realized that. Indiw wove to the edge of the pattern and went after Falstaff.

The human got one of the porkies with a cannon shot, and Indiw used his last porky buster on another. The Ardr pilot, shaken loose from the box he'd been trapped in, pounded away at one of the two remaining porkies.

Indiw approached from behind him and, warning "Shihay, break," fired point-blank into the opening gunport of the porky. The Ardr slid aside to avoid Indiw's shot. The porky became a massive ball of fire. The Ardr called, "Indiw? Neighbor's salute. Bpikim here."

"Bpikim. Should have known it was you. Apologies about that human's timing."

"I shouldn't have said that about dunking him."

"True. Humans wouldn't understand."

"Why not?"

"Bpikim, you don't want to know!"

"Still, I should just have said I'd gut him and have done with it. He's pretty amazing. Never heard of a human who could weave pattern. Did you teach him?"

Loaded question. "No! They have a simulator program he became addicted to." As they spoke, Indiw had been scanning the particle fog for Falstaff's transponder, getting anxious. "Where did he go?"

"There!"

Indiw followed Bpikim to where Falstaff had engaged two fighters and the last of the four porkies. The three Hyos blocked their way back to the Ardr pattern. Bpikim called the break.

Amazingly, Falstaff dove under the fighter he was attacking just as Bpikim whipped his slicer across the Hyos. With the Hyos's shields adjusted to repel the slicer, Indiw hit him with a cannon shot, then swerved away to where he hoped Falstaff would be. Meanwhile, Bpikim had swooped over the Hyos and lashed out at the other fighter while dodging the porky's cannon shots.

The human fell in behind Indiw, saying, "Glad I remembered that pattern call!"

"Here's the next one." Indiw explained the maneuver and cautioned him, "Just don't fire to your left and maybe you won't hit my neighbor Bpikim."

"The guy I almost scragged? Your neighbor?"

"Here he comes. Break."

The weave brought both porkies together determined to get the Ardr vermin no matter what. Swatting at the dancing images of Ardr all around them, they shot their own fighter out of space.

Falstaff killed one porky while Indiw got the other.

"You didn't leave any for me," said Bpikim on the human band and in the language used most on *Tacoma*. He was flying one of *Tacoma*'s fighters and had switched on his com scanner.

"There's plenty more," said Falstaff. "By the way. Apologies."

"Accepted. This time. Ready, Indiw? Break."

They streaked back to the pattern just in time to join the tail end. Bpikim wove adroitly into the center. Indiw kept Falstaff at the edge and wove them toward the underside of the pattern. They were penetrating the shell of the globe at a good pace. Indiw checked behind them and found a solid wall of Hyos. But none were trying to engage the advancing Ardr. "Tagawa's behind us, keeping them busy!" said Indiw.

"I think you're right. She must have been given orders to do it again. Probably the other wings are converging from either side."

"Good. We'll all meet in the center."

But it didn't work that way.

It wasn't true that the Hyos never learn.

Once Sinaha's defenders were deep into the crust of the globular formation and unable to disengage, the whole huge globe expanded. That gave more space between ships to maneuver, but also allowed the Hyos to surround all the human attackers.

Then another smaller, tightly formed globular formation of Hyos emerged from the center of the swollen globe. Right below the Ardr formation, the crust of the globe cracked open to let the smaller formation emerge.

Uyitin's voice identified the fugitive globe, "The Breeder ship! Anyone who can get free! After them!"

"Falstaff—straight line. Break!"

Indiw dove straight down into the crack, piling on everything he had short of lightspeed transition. The internal gravity overloaded and he took four times Sinaha's gravity, but he shot through the crack in the Hyos globe just as it closed up behind him.

Decelerating hard, he paused to look around. Falstaff pulled up at his side, though the human was gasping and unable to answer the com check. Humans couldn't take high gravity for long. Eight Ardr had made it through the crack behind him. As he watched, a handful of human fighters emerged from the large globe fighting for every handsbreadth of progress into the clear.

"All squadrons, form on me," said Tagawa's voice. Her craft's transponder put a flashing star on everyone's tactical display. Indiw ignored it.

Falstaff said, "We should help them."

"There's the Breeder ship! I'm going after it."

The other Ardr had assembled a pattern. They arrowed after the small globe of Hyos, streaking directly for Sinaha.

Indiw was astonished at how close they were to the planet. He blended into the edge of the Ardr pattern, Falstaff straggling behind. "Pit Bull Four. Do you have damage, Pit Bull Three?"

"Not too much," answered Falstaff. "That power dive about did me in, but the craft's all right. Yourself?"

"Spaceworthy."

"That's not battleworthy."

"Might be." There was a lot of red on his board.

"A judgment call, huh?"

"Something like that."

They reached the outermost fringes of atmosphere. Turbulence slowed the Hyos fighters. The bigger, clumsier Breeder ship bounced and jigged. The Ardr punched ahead at full speed until they caught up with the rear guard of the Breeder ship's protectors.

Suddenly, battle raged hot and fierce all around. Indiw ignored it and pushed through toward the Breeder. Never had the Hyos gotten so close to his planet—his land. If that ship reached ground, the First Tier would cede the planet and leave them all to die. It had happened before on other borders with the Hyos.

No!

But it was all too likely. His tactical displays now picked up the status transponder from Sinaha ground defense. It

showed the planetary defenses riddled with huge holes—
the work, no doubt, of the Hyos that came in with *Int**.

They dove deep into atmosphere, the drag altering the
way his craft handled, the gravity straining the seams more
with every maneuver, heat building on the hull. He battered
his way past the last Hyos fighter and into the center of the
protective globe.

And there it was. The Breeder ship.

It was a needle-nosed, wedge-shaped atmosphere craft
built to land in any terrain. It could even splash down on
open ocean and take off again to make landfall as per the
treaty. Its speed and maneuverability in atmosphere would
exceed anything a space fighter could achieve.

It carried nothing but the small number of fertile individuals who made up the heart of a Hyos swarm. All the
rest of the craft was devoted to radiation shielding and
crash padding. Some Breeders, especially of large swarms,
also carried cryogenically suspended germ plasm and even
developed zygotes and fetuses. Without that ship, the Hyos
were incapable of reproduction.

Indiw drove for his target, running all the energy he could
spare into recharging his cannon. To his right, something
exploded, buffeting him off course. He ignored it and corrected. Below him, a Hyos fired upward into his still solid
lower shielding. He didn't return fire.

The Breeder's sensors raked over him, setting off alarms.
It speeded up, outstripping its fighter escort, running from
him. Alone. It was his!

Instruments registered a momentary slicer lock seizing
him from behind. His shields greened out. Then debris
showered over him. He lost the Breeder behind the veil
of static that flowed over his badly distorted readouts. His
instruments were failing, but he would get one good shot
and that would be all he needed.

A Hyos fighter loomed ahead of him.

Indiw dove under it. It exploded behind him. The atmosphere transmitted the shock wave, sending him tumbling
out of control.

He came out of it skimming the peaks of a mountain

range. The Breeder ship was ahead of him, too far away for
an atmosphere shot. His cannon charge still held, redlined
above the maximum. It would pack a terrific wallop. It
might very well turn him into a particle storm. Or the heat
of that shot in atmosphere might fry every sensor mounted
on his craft's skin. He would get only one chance.

But the monitors had a huge safety factor built in. They
never read true.

Pushing his speed way past the safety zones, he gradually closed on his quarry. Behind him, Falstaff and a six-
member squadron formation began losing ground. Above
them danced the remaining Ardr who had gotten out with
him. It was sobering that the fate of their land rested entirely
on his piloting. Atmosphere piloting at that.

A moment later he was slanting down the eastern slope of
the mountain range. A huge fertile plain spread before him,
carved into living zones, each one rimmed by Walkways
and hatcheries nestled against the curves in the meandering river.

He didn't need his mapper display to know exactly where
he was. It didn't make any difference that it was on the other
side of the planet from his own land. If that Breeder went to
ground here, the whole planet was lost.

He turned off his gravity compensators, shifting all their
energy into his drive. He had to close the gap to the Breeder
ship. Below the telltale puffs marked ground-based ordnance of the individual land holders trying for the Breeder.
The Breeder's shields flared, fending off the near misses
easily. But those shields would *not* hold against his cannon.
They would *not*!

A sudden direct hit turned the Breeder into a bright white
globe for a moment, and Indiw thought it was gone. But the
brightness cleared and the Breeder had gained speed. Indiw
piled on acceleration.

It pushed him back into his seat viciously. But he was
gaining. Not fast enough. Just not fast enough.

Without warning, the Breeder slewed to the left, skimmed
lower, whipped into a right turn around a butte and disappeared.

And he knew why. It had slowed to land expecting him to overshoot the mark and lose his one chance.

He reversed thrust, hauling his shuddering, screaming, glowing craft around in a turn it was never designed to make. The fighter bucked, fought the controls, heeled over, and inverted. He righted himself, found the horizon, and vectored onto the course circling left around the far side of the butte. He trailed booming shock waves cruel to those below. They'd thank him if he made it. But he might not. The turn was too wide. He'd have a long, long run on the straight leg back to target, giving them plenty of time to land and broadcast their claim.

Behind the butte, the map showed the river curled into a broad turn leaving a wide sandy strip perfect for a landing.

Falstaff's voice startled him. "Go for it, Pit Bull Four! We'll cover you."

Flanking him on either side were Pit Bull Three and Captain Tagawa. His wake buffeted them hard, but they held position.

And then they were around the butte and leveling off for the run back toward the landing site.

The Breeder was already on the ground.

Their broadcast rammed through all the static, coming through so loud it hurt, simultaneously reaching through deep space to First Tier relay points and thus to all the worlds of the alliance. It was couched in the formal language of the treaty.

"Hyos Swarm Shikto. Claim this planet once called Sinaha, Ardr possession. Treaty term completed. Cede immediately or die."

Indiw heard nothing but the extreme gloating pleasure in the alien voice. *No!* "No! This is *my* land!"

His targeting program acquired the Breeder. He slammed home the lock, put every bit of power into thrust, and committed everything to ridding his land of the intruder.

Rage boiled up, obliterating judgment. It was rage held since the moment he'd spared Falstaff's life, primal rage, rage that could not be denied.

Suddenly a human craft was ahead of him, slowing, shields intruding between his cannon and the target. Tagawa's voice screamed in his ear, "Abort! Pull up, Pit Bull Four. Pull up or I'll ram you!"

"Captain, no!" came Falstaff's voice. "He's not going to quit! He *can't.*"

Falstaff understood.

A human could understand. It was a revelation. And with that, sanity returned. If he delivered that cannon shot from a human ship—not from his own land—the treaty would be broken. It would be all-out war with the Hyos, a war that this time could only end in genocide. Which side would die was by no means certain.

His instrument board flashed as Tagawa's cannon tracer locked on to him. "Abort or I'll take you out!"

He held, trying to make up his mind.

Falstaff groaned, "Captain, no!"

"He's insane," she sneered.

"Indiw!" pleaded Falstaff.

Indiw held course and target lock until the very edge of his shields touched Tagawa's. If there was one lesson he had learned and learned well, all the way down to the instinctive level, it was that human females were the most dangerous creatures in the galaxy. She would die with him to prevent his shot. If he blasted the Breeder, he'd lose his land to the fury of total war. If he didn't, it was lost anyway.

There was nothing to gain.

"Aaakhkhkh!" he howled.

With alarms shrieking and circuits smoking as the shields interpenetrated, Indiw pulled into a vertical climb.

A few seconds later he blacked out. He'd forgotten he had disabled his gravity controls.

He came to at orbital height, Falstaff and Tagawa laboring to close the gap with him.

"Down!" ordered Tagawa. "We'll land at that public field on the other side of the planet. They'll have orbiting capsules full of refugees for us to lift to *Tacoma*. Falstaff, tell *Tacoma* we stopped him. Commander Indiw, don't you dare deviate from course or I'll shoot you out of the sky. You got that, mister?"

"I understand you, Captain Tagawa."

Falstaff said, "Indiw, agree to obey her orders until we get back to *Tacoma.*" At Indiw's silence, he added, "Come on, buddy, don't make me a party to killing you!"

Cold sanity had returned full force. He had failed. Nothing but blackness stretched before him.

He heard his voice say, "I agree."

Tagawa's sigh gusted through the speakers. "Falstaff, get through to *Tacoma.* Now."

There was a click, and suddenly Tagawa's voice was coming through on the Ardr band. She was hailing ground control at the public landing field.

There were indeed refugees assembling, the unlanded abandoning the planet. The landed would die with their land. It was a privilege his human friend and the female had denied him. Dimly, it came to him that the punishment was no more than he deserved for his failure.

The rest of that long orbital slide into the public landing field passed in a fog. To the end of his days, Indiw never remembered the sequence of events clearly. But later, they told him that he'd landed his craft in perfect formation with the two humans. Together with a number of other humans and a few surviving Ardr, he'd ferried refugee capsules up to *Tacoma.*

On his last trip, he'd delivered his tow safely into the landing bay and then had crashed into the safety fields, without a single grain of fuel left. He never remembered that, either, not even when he saw the recording.

Meanwhile, unknown to him, the big carrier had gathered up all its own stray survivors and jettisoned matériel, formally ceded the system to the Hyos, and headed at flank speed toward Aberdeen.

But they were too late. Aberdeen had been lost. Halfway there, they met hundreds of small craft, mostly in-system craft not rated for deep space. Refugees. They collected every living being they could find, no matter that there was no room left on the great carrier.

Every bit of floor space was crammed with living flesh. The offices, the gym, the mess halls, the kitchens, sickbay, an empty food locker, cargo bays, the recreation deck, the repair docks, and at the last the flight decks themselves. Even the Captain's office domiciled a family of eight, and four couples took up residence on the bridge.

Satisfied that there wasn't another living being in the flotsam around them, *Tacoma* made for the inner systems of the First Tier Alliance, broadcasting a plea for help that even the Fornak would not deny.

But it was eight days before help arrived.

The air became foul. Dozens suffocated in pockets of uncirculated air. Others died from the strain of oxygen deprivation or carbon dioxide overload. Disease began to spread. There was nothing much the medical department could do. The brutal rules of triage applied. What little water was rationed out to each person for drinking was vile with not-quite-recycled waste.

The Ardr foodstuffs ran out on the fifth day. Humans were rationed to one-third survival minimum by the second day. Tempers frayed, flared.

At first the sporadic violence was confined among each species, but then on the fifth day, an Ardr gutted a human child. The riot killed eighty people. The police action that stopped it killed fifty more. That didn't relieve the crowding one whit.

But Indiw knew none of this. It was just as well. He wasn't rational. He'd have been one of those to blood his claws in human flesh. The stench of densely packed, starving, scared bodies would have been enough to do it. He was the only ex-landed Ardr aboard. And he was responsible for all this.

On the sixth day, they got word of the approaching armada that would take off all the Ardr refugees and some of the humans. It was a ragtag collection of craft, anything that could hold atmosphere and deliver supplies to *Tacoma.*

The first refugees were transferred off *Tacoma* near the end of the eighth day, and the job was finished by late afternoon of the ninth. They were still finding rotting bodies in closets and corners on the tenth day. Two days later, even though *Tacoma* was still technically overloaded with humans, the air became breathable, and the disgusting taint faded from the water supply.

It was only then that Indiw drifted slowly back into awareness.

★
CHAPTER
TEN

★

THERE WERE FOUR HUMANS IN HIS QUARTERS WITH him.

All his senses told him this was so, though it could not be. Yet he felt the pressure on his skin, on his horns, and especially the smell. Even the heat of the human bodies washed against him unpleasantly despite the artificial sap tree over his sand bed.

He forced his eyes open, certain that would clear away the nightmarish *presence*. The lighting was reassuringly normal, though images blurred into one another, and even separated into two copies, then rejoined into one.

Gradually, his vision cleared and his mind focused, dispelling the aura of hallucination. Stark reality was worse.

A human female adult was seated on the floor, back propped against the corner to the right of the entry. A female adolescent lay across her thighs, sleeping. *Two human females! In my place!* Alarm spread through him leaving weak trembling in its wake. He shifted to relieve cramped muscles and two more humans came into his field of view.

A male adolescent bent over Indiw's desk screen. Ray Falstaff crouched over the boy and directed him in the solving of some problem. In profile, the boy had the ineffable Falstaff nose jutting out from under the light-transforming goggles all four humans wore to compensate for the Ardr spectrum in his quarters.

Another Falstaff! The nightmare feeling returned.

"Ray, he's awake." The woman's voice was soft, a mere whisper, but it cut through Indiw's nerves like cold steel.

Falstaff turned. "Indiw! Do you know who I am? Do you know where you are now?"

Indiw jerked his head in the human affirmative, eyes riveted to the human.

"Thank God! You see, Mom, I was right! He's going to make it. Indiw"—he stepped toward the sand bed—"we had four different Ardr physicians working on you. They all agreed you'd never come out of it. They wanted to heave you out an airlock to save air, but I wouldn't give up. I made them show me how to care for you. And I was right. You're going to be fine now."

Falstaff took another couple of steps closer. "I thought, since there was no alternative, that you'd prefer to have us rather than total strangers in here. That's my mother and my sister Marg, and this is Kevin, my brother. Sometimes we call him Buddy."

These were the children Walter Falstaff had thought of as his own progeny. It made Indiw's skin crawl, and if he'd had anything in his stomach, he knew he'd have lost every bit of it catastrophically. Worse yet, one of the children was female—a female Falstaff! And she was looking at him. Hard.

Falstaff was only two paces away. Indiw wrenched himself over to face the bulkhead and curled with his back to the human, groaning his pain and misery, his need for solitude overwhelming him.

"There's no place else for us to go, Indiw," said Falstaff as if Indiw had spoken aloud. "There're eight people in my cabin. Every wide spot in the halls has people camped in it. There's a curfew—nobody allowed out of their assigned place for the next ten hours. There have been some bad fights. Really bad."

Indiw just nodded, clenched his fists until his claws bit into his palms, and hunkered down to endure. Falstaff sat beside him, murmuring softly, recounting the whole ghastly scenario that Indiw had missed, promising that they'd leave him alone to eat and bathe as soon as curfew allowed, offering every kindness the human could think of.

Indiw endured, struggling not to vocalize his anguished misery, determined not to disgrace himself. Once again, he owed life itself to a Falstaff—a number of Falstaffs. Every sense told him they weren't enjoying this any more than he was—less maybe, for they realized he could go berserk and gut the lot of them before they knew what had happened.

And as bad as it was, with every passing breath, he realized that, despite everything, despite his losses, despite his new status as an ex-landed pariah, he wanted to live. That was a shocking revelation.

Eventually the four humans left for the mess hall promising to stay away as long as possible. They were gone for six hours, which Indiw put to good use. Wobbly as his legs were, he tended his personal needs, cleaned the bed, and de-scented the place as best he could.

With a stomach full of the field rations *Tacoma* had been resupplied with, he felt better. His intellectual appreciation of what Falstaff had done for him began to seep through into his emotions. He couldn't blame the human because, after all, Ray Falstaff had no way to grasp the sheer asinine stupidity of his choice.

Ray Falstaff returned before the others that first day that Indiw remembered. He sounded the door signal and, when Indiw opened the door, stood beyond the threshold tentatively. The diffidence, the politeness, touched Indiw deeply. He stood aside, gesturing the human to enter. "It's a public place now."

Falstaff stepped in carefully and moved away to give Indiw space. "Indiw, I'm sorry. I know you'd have preferred to die. But I couldn't—let it happen. I just couldn't."

"Why?" The question was equal parts curiosity and complaint, lightly laced with a marveling gratitude.

Falstaff shrugged. "You're Pit Bull Squadron. My wingman. My friend. You spared my life against every instinct you own. You're the best pilot I know of. Or maybe just because you called me neighbor and let me call you friend without saying you could never be anything of the sort—which we both know is true. Good God, Indiw, I wanted to take out that damn Breeder ship as much as you did!"

"Why didn't you?"

"Because by the treaty, they had already become 'settled' Hyos, legal residents of the planet. To fire on them would have been to fire on the whole Hyos Empire, and we don't even know for sure how big that is!"

"You would have blown me to pieces if Tagawa had ordered you to."

Falstaff turned and their eyes locked. "No! Believe it, Indiw, I'd have found another way." His voice shook with passion. "You're Pit Bull Squadron. Sometimes, that's closer than family."

Stricken at that thought, Indiw turned away.

"Oh, shit, I didn't mean that the way it sounded."

"My faulty judgment has lost an entire planet. There is nowhere among Ardr that I can move without expecting to be attacked and killed without warning. And yet you still accept me as worthy of life. It is a bizarre twist."

"Faulty judgment? Indiw, blowing up a grounded Breeder ship while it's broadcasting a planetary claim would have been the worst judgment of all. Surely your people wouldn't kill you for obeying the treaty!"

He sighed. "No, not for obeying the treaty. For not having nailed the Breeder while it was still in the air—or, better yet, space. Or, having failed, then for not returning to my land to defend it to the death. Tagawa prevented even that."

"Oh, Indiw, you rescued at least a hundred people in those last couple of hours! You're a—oh, damn, you don't want to know what that makes you."

"A hero?"

"I didn't say it, you did."

"The rescue is irrelevant. Those people were unlanded. Those who survived will only move inward to more heavily settled territory and vie for land against those who have a greater right to it. The unlanded, however, are held in higher regard than I."

"After all you've accomplished?"

He tried to explain. But Falstaff simply couldn't grasp it. In the end, he advised the human, "Just take it that there is no place in Ardr society for one who holds the privileges of the landed but is possessed by the gnawing hunger for land. An ex-landed Ardr is a danger to the stability of civilization and will quickly kill or be killed. And if he wins land in a challenge, it is not likely he'd ever be accepted as a neighbor. His judgment is obviously faulty even if his strength is great. Such a land holder will be challenged often and soon lose."

And such a land holder would never be chosen on the Walkway just as an ex-landed Ardr would never be allowed to enter a Walkway. It was the first time the thought had occurred to him. He'd never know a female's touch again.

Falstaff paced, nodding, "So that's why the physicians all thought it would be kinder to stuff you out an airlock."

"That's why." *He'd never understand.*

"Were they right?"

"I don't know." *Yes!*

"Well, as long as you're in doubt, I'm winning."

"Winning? What contest?"

"To keep the best goddamned wingman in the Service!"

"Keep?" He must have missed something.

"Well, so what if you can't fly with the Ardr wings? You've got a place on *Tacoma.* You've got your commission, back pay worth a bundle, 'Above and Beyond' bonuses, a few decorations, and a promotion if you'll take it. Not only that, but you've got the pure, unadulterated respect of every pilot on this ship."

"Except Captain Tagawa."

"Well, we can work on that, too."

"Ray, I've violated so many of your rules I can't even count them all. And I don't regret it. I'm surprised I didn't wake up in the brig."

"It was taken over by Medical for an isolation ward."

They looked at each other for a long, stretched-out moment, and then simultaneously burst out laughing.

What had happened on this ship was nothing to laugh about. Indiw's position was nothing to laugh about. And yet, they laughed, and it felt very good. When it was over, there was a long, quiet stretch, and then Falstaff said, "I'm going to go take a shower before the womenfolk get here."

That became the theme song for the next couple of days, the men vying for the facilities before the women-folk took over. Watching the human family nursing their traumas and straining to act normally, Indiw reaffirmed his view of human females a thousand times. Never once did Ray contradict his mother, never once did he preempt the facilities, a chair, or the desk screen when his sister wanted them. However, he contested everything with his brother.

Once, Indiw came in after taking a restless turn around the overcrowded ship's corridors to find Ray and Kevin rolling on the deck, kicking and punching. Kevin was screaming abusive threats. Ray was laughing in a tone Indiw had never heard him use.

They froze when he entered. Then Ray threw one last punch and pulled his brother to his feet. "It's okay, it's just Indiw. I won't tell Mom if you don't."

"Deal," said Kevin quickly.

They shook hands and the younger Falstaff went into the facilities to repair the damage to his appearance. Indiw stared at the deck where the two had fought. He'd seen Ray Falstaff in deadly combat. The spindly armed boy could not have lasted five seconds against the man. The mother wouldn't have made it two seconds. Yet both males feared her wrath more than anything else in life.

Ray saw his puzzlement and offered, "Look, he's my little brother, okay?"

"If you say so." Indiw took a lap reader and retreated to the farthest corner of his sand bed, the only little square patch of the universe that was his alone.

"Indiw, I'd give my life for that kid. I'd never hurt him. I'd kill anyone who tried. But I'm not going to let him get away with anything, either." His voice choked up, and very hoarsely, he whispered, "He's going to grow up strong."

"I understand. He's your identity as my land was my identity. I won't touch him."

"I never thought you would!" Shaking his head, he let Indiw retreat into his reading.

Late that night, while the lighting was turned down to its dimmest setting, Indiw woke to a strange, arrhythmic sound. It came from the corner where the mother slept holding the young female. Alarmed that some remnant of the illnesses that had stalked the ship still remained, he sat up to peer across the room. But even as he searched for the cause, Ray Falstaff scrambled across the floor from where he shared blankets with his brother.

"Mom? Marg? Oh, damn. You *had* to leave her. She's gone, Mom, the Hyos killed her. You did the right thing to leave her there."

"The Hyos will b-burn her body! She'll never get a proper burial. Your father would have wanted her to be buried!" And then the sobbing resumed, louder, more uncontrolled.

He recognized grief, and Ray's forlorn attempts at comfort. Indiw, too, was in mourning for his losses, cut off from the solitude he needed as this woman was cut off from the burial custom she needed.

In the course of the long, agonizing session, Indiw learned that the Falstaffs had seen their youngest child die, and that was a source of incredibly deep pain that knew no comfort or surcease. But they had also lost others dear to them, whose fate they didn't know.

Finally, sleep came to them. And in the morning, there was a sort of brittle, forced cheer donned for his sake—or perhaps to guard their privacy from a stranger.

He never mentioned what he'd overheard, but he crept carefully around the adult female, unsure what kind of berserk rage might erupt from one who struggled in such bereavement. But if it terrified those who knew her best, surely it would be something he couldn't handle.

The tension in the tiny compartment grew rapidly after that, but less than two days later, they arrived at Ygnacio.

The refugees were off-loaded onto tenders that met *Tacoma* far outside the system, where they first dropped below lightspeed. Ray's parting from his family was almost as anguished as that single night-long session Indiw had witnessed. But Ygnacio's social machinery had engaged to welcome the refugees and offer them security, noble status, and aid for their emotional traumas.

Apparently, inner-system humans admired those who had tried to pioneer on the borders of the alliance, even if they returned in failure. Without fanfare, they had become honored members of a new pack.

As the last of the refugees were departing, Falstaff moved back into his own quarters, as did all the others who had moved to make room for refugees. Suddenly, on the pilot's deck, there were a lot of empty rooms, empty slots for nameplates beside the doors. The silence was eerie.

Tacoma took the last leg of the trip into the Ygnacio system at a leisurely pace, every hand turned out to clean and polish every surface on the ship. Even Indiw was assigned a section of floor to scrub in a public corridor where the automatic cleaning machinery had been cannibalized by Environmental for water recycling.

They arrived at Ygnacio Station ready for an Admiral's inspection in everything but supply inventory. The sound, smell, feel, and spirit of the ship almost seemed normal again. The familiarity of that was oddly piercing.

Indiw had his own place once again in perfect order, though he'd been personally assured by Captain Reid that any inspection would not include requiring him even to open the door to his quarters, never mind to admit someone. *Tacoma*'s Captain had stated that Indiw had endured more than his fair share of indignities and had acquitted himself as an officer and a gentleman. Then he'd hastily apologized in case that seemed like an offensive remark.

There were several similar incidents where the humans went out of their way to accommodate the alien among them. Considering how he'd blithely ignored his obligations to their rules and regulations, it was severely puzzling.

When he asked Falstaff, the human just grinned and said, "You'll see."

A few hours after they berthed at Ygnacio Station, they stood to inspection. Indiw wore the Commander's uniform. True to Reid's word, though all the other pilots stood before their open doors, Indiw was not required to open his for the prying eyes. Other cabins were entered, but no one even touched the door of Indiw's.

The six impeccably clad, gold-braided officers who marched through the pilots' deck barked contentious challenges at the human pilots, but one of them addressed him politely in an Ardr dialect, saying only, "You have earned all consideration among us. Your judgment is endorsed."

Indiw doubted he meant it, doubted he even knew what it meant. But it warmed him incredibly to hear the words, however badly pronounced. "I have found much to admire among you."

"Good. You may find much more with time."

Indiw puzzled over that all the rest of the afternoon and throughout the evening ceremonies. He was not required to attend the formal dining ceremony in the large mess, nor did anyone threaten him with citations of merit, medals of valor, or any other distinguishing award. He was left alone all during the memorial ceremonies held the following day.

But he didn't feel excluded. Quite the contrary. Captain Lorton relayed Captain Reid's invitation to fly the missing-man formation over Ygnacio's major cities where the refugees were now domiciled. Memorial ceremonies were in progress there all day as well.

Even though there were probably no Ardr on the planet, he had declined the honor, and that had been accepted without comment. He had spent the day in his own place, luxuriating in the wonderful solitude, at last able to grieve for his lost life.

Orders arrived on his desk during the late afternoon. Worded as a polite request, the summons called him to a meeting in Captain Reid's briefing room at the beginning of first watch. There was no hint of the purpose of the meeting, no list of who else would be there.

But Indiw thought he knew what it would be about. The moment of reckoning was at hand. The fist of human justice was about to squeeze him to a pulp. Politely.

He pondered, changed his mind three times, and finally elected to present himself in the Commander's uniform. He had not yet officially resigned. The Records Office had only opened for business again just before the inspection. As he understood it, eighty people had been domiciled in that office during the retreat.

Besides, since he was being summoned to a court-martial, he should wear the appropriate attire.

He found the place this time without any help. Captain Reid was standing outside his briefing-room door waiting for him. He was the last to arrive. At least he'd done *that* right. If they all viewed him as guilty, perhaps they'd take his good timing into account.

Reid closed the door behind Indiw and stepped to the front of the long table.

Before Indiw could move, Captain Tagawa came up to him, stepping too close for comfort, braced in that unnaturally erect posture humans used. "Commander Indiw, I owe you the most abject apology. For the last three weeks, half the people on this ship have been making me understand what I must have looked like from your point of view. It's not—a flattering image. Can't we start over—try to establish a more respectful working relationship?"

She stood back, having delivered a rehearsed speech, and waited as if her career advancement depended on his acceptance. It was a unique experience, seeing a human female at his mercy. But the Falstaffs had taught him well what care one must take around a human female, especially one who feels temporarily beaten.

Instead of casually gutting her on the spot, he took one step backward, hands behind his back, and bowed low enough to present his horns to her mercy. "I would be honored for a second chance to earn your regard."

Her eyes darted to Captain Reid, then back to Indiw. "Then—no hard feelings, Commander. Let's get to work."

As she moved around the table to the end of the room where Reid stood, Indiw had another blinding insight about humans. Their survival mechanism was not judgment, as with Ardr. The human species survival mechanism was their lack of a survival mechanism. All the books said humans had retained no instincts. You couldn't even count on their xenophobia, the closest thing to an instinct left in their genes!

He turned his attention to the room itself, suddenly more apprehensive than he'd ever been before. The viewscreen at the far end of the room was blank. There were no drinks or foodstuffs on the table. The chair at the end of the table near the door had been adjusted for Ardr proportions, and Reid gestured him to it.

Determined not to show how unsettled he was by his new insight, he sat. Why did they put themselves out for him when their code required them to punish rule breakers? Maybe he didn't understand the concept of rules?

At Reid's end of the table Lorton, his two women, Falstaff, and Tagawa grouped themselves around Reid, Reid's aides, and some others, probably replacements of Wing Captains who hadn't survived. If he read the insignias correctly, the man next to Falstaff was the new interspecies Protocol Officer. That could account for some of the more bewildering actions of the humans, but not for their motives in going to all that trouble for his sake.

Reid touched a switch set into the table. "This room is now secured. You have all filed updated security pledges. Nothing we say here will leave this room." The Protocol Officer muttered something to Reid. Reid continued, "Commander Indiw, that means that you signed an agreement not to discuss classified matters—it was in connection with another project, but it covers this as well. Do you understand and agree?"

"I understand and agree."

"Good. Our battle recordings of the losses of the planets Sinaha, Aberdeen, and Thait*o are still being reviewed. However, preliminary reports were sent up the chain of command while we were en route. This is the part that must not be mentioned outside this room.

"It appears—*appears*—that there may have been a massive, blatant violation of the Hyos/Tier/Treaty by the settled Hyos. It may be very, very hard to prove, but it is suspected that the settled Hyos on their side of the border have provided resources to the forming swarms far in excess of treaty limits. It may even be that the settled Hyos used their resources to link the swarms from their border planets with swarms formed in the interior of their empire.

"That would be flagrant violation of the letter of the treaty. The swarms' sudden acquisition of high-level intelligence is attributed to their access to the diplomatic channels of the settled Hyos.

"If all that is proved, or if the suspicion is so strong final proof is waived, then we will be part of the task force sent to retake Thait*o, Sinaha, and Aberdeen, risking total war with the settled Hyos Empire.

"For weeks now, diplomatic messages have been flying at the highest levels. So far, no result. But they can't keep this under wraps for much longer. It's going to hit the press soon, and then the Hyos will know we're on our way. We have to be set to move at a moment's notice.

"And this ship is far, far from ready. That's why I called you all here today. To impress on you the importance of your jobs, and to make sure that I have your total cooperation."

There was a general grumble of agreement. But they were also puzzled. The information did not seem to be the sort of thing that would be divulged to people who would do their jobs anyway.

Reid held up his hand for silence. "There's more to this than the Hyos. As you all know, the First Tier Alliance is an uneasy one. We've all had our noses rubbed in just how uneasy it is, with what's gone on aboard this ship while it was crammed with refugees. Even under primary survival pressure, with the strongest of all possible motivations, humans and Ardr couldn't keep from killing one another for no particular reason except misunderstanding and bad manners.

"Imagine what would have happened had there been Fornak aboard as well!

"Not only that, but my very best fighter pilot almost got himself court-martialed for upholding the highest possible moral standard his species knows. I'm talking about you, Indiw. You did know you were in trouble, didn't you?"

"Yes, Captain, I knew. I still don't understand what's going on here."

"What's going on here is a publicity stunt. Your presence on this ship and your performance during the last battle of Sinaha has attracted attention at the highest levels. *Tacoma* has become a laboratory of interspecies relationships. You are the first Ardr ever to consent to work among humans. Surely you knew that?"

"Yes, Captain." Indiw restrained the urge to squirm.

Reid met Indiw's gaze steadily. "I have been ordered to make sure that we take every possible advantage of your presence, that we learn how to work with you, and that as a result, *Tacoma* will become living proof that humans and Ardr are natural allies.

"Your stunt with using the Ardr pattern weave around a human formation saved more than a hundred lives, and won a battle. The Admiralty is anxious to prove that the closer humans and Ardr work together, the stronger we are. If it comes to another all-out war against the Hyos, then we must integrate our forces deeply—Ardr, Fornak, and humans must live and work on the same ships, respond to the same command structure, and fight as a single unified force.

"If we are so rigid in our way of doing things that we can't make room for one Ardr—who is one helluva terrific pilot—then that war against the Hyos is lost before it starts.

"I've had it explained to me seven ways from Sunday that if you're forced into the limelight, you'll lose every bit of the high regard you've won among your own people, and everything we intend to accomplish here will be lost. So our appreciation for your work will be evident only in your paycheck. Is that acceptable to you?"

"Well, yes, but—"

"Now don't tell me again that you intend to resign your commission. Surely, you can see that this is the right place for you to serve in this war."

"I'm not held in high regard by my people. There is nothing to be gained by my serving on this ship."

"To the contrary. If we do recapture Sinaha, your land will be returned to you and your judgment vindicated. No?"

That was a definite possibility.

"And if we recapture Sinaha, that's when the war will start. No?"

Indiw nodded.

"If you resign and leave *Tacoma*, what are your chances of serving on a ship that will be sent to recapture Sinaha?"

"Not good."

Quietly, as if he knew what he was asking, Reid said, "You want to go fight for your land, Indiw?"

"Yes."

"Then come with us. Help us forge a new link in our alliance. You can choose who to work with, who to fly with, whose orders you agree to follow on whatever conditions you set, and you can pick out your own jobs on the ship— teach, do engineering, research, piloting, any or all jobs *you* judge you're qualified for. We're going to trust your judgment and take your word for it when you agree to do a job, and we want to earn your trust. Will you give us a chance?"

There was no way to turn it down. But he might be remembered as the first Ardr who betrayed his own kind to the pack hunters who had become the scourge of the galaxy. Or maybe he'd be remembered as the one who averted the threat by proving the Ardr to be the natural ally of the humans.

"I will stay to retake Sinaha. After that, I expect to resign and go home."

"Fair enough."

To the others at the table, Reid said, "The code name for the species-integration project is Gemini Twins because

Walter Falstaff was the identical twin of Raymond Falstaff's father. Every detail of the operation is under top security wrap. Indiw, if anyone steps on your—ah—toe claws, you come directly to me and discuss it only in a secured room. Is that clear?"

"Yes."

"I mean, do you agree?"

"Yes. I agree."

Indiw remembered the U-shaped diagram that had been labeled as the constellation Gemini in the Earth sky. There had been a story about twins, Castor and Pollux. They had been inseparable, participating in the most heroic events of their time. But they had not been identical twins. They had different fathers, but the same mother. And the fathers had been of different species. One of the fathers had made the twins into stars.

He didn't like that code name at all. He didn't like anything about this situation except that suddenly he might get his land back. Whatever the cost, it would not be too much. He spent the rest of the meeting visualizing his waterfall, his swamp, his Walkway, his female neighbors. He was going home. Soon. That is, if the humans, collectively, were as formidable as he'd begun to suspect they might be.

On that night of the first Hyos attack, he had thought he'd have to admit to all of Sinaha that he'd been wrong, that human pack-hunter nature would indeed compel the aliens to wipe out the lone-hunter Ardr. He'd been on the verge of publicly admitting his mistake. But he'd grasped only part of the truth. Humans were not just pack hunters evolving into individuals. Each individual hunted with their ancestors and their progeny. They didn't preserve their own lives and lands, they preserved their *traditions* to link them to their past and their future.

Clearly, Indiw's role in Operation Gemini Twins was to keep the human ferocity targeted on the Hyos and away from Ardr. Only as long as the Hyos survived would the Ardr be safe. If the Hyos survived long enough, perhaps the humans would come to regard alliance with Ardr as a tradition to be preserved. That would create a precarious safety of sorts.

As the meeting broke up, Falstaff caught his eye, held his gaze for a moment, then flashed him a huge grin and stuck one thumb in the air. "Pit Bull Squadron rises again!"

Indiw had seen that gesture many times before. He wondered if it was as lewd as it looked. He hoped so as he returned it with a grin.

ABOUT THE AUTHOR

Daniel R. Kerns loves archery, riflery, deep-sea fishing, golf, photography, hiking, and beachcombing, but not as much as reading sf novels. Youthful fascination with the writings of Hal Clement, Murray Leinster, Isaac Asimov, Edward E. Smith, and Robert Heinlein has expanded to include martial arts and vintage movies about war, spies, and intrigue.

The idea for the Ardr Universe crystallized at the Air Force commissioning of Kerns's youngest child. The request for one sequel to *Hero* instantly produced plot outlines for not one but three more Pit Bull Squadron novels. It looks like this hobby has turned into a career.